HORIZON

APEX PREDATOR

M. T. ANDERSON

WITHDRAWN

SCHOLASTIC INC.

Library of Congress Control Number: 2018943241

ISBN 978-1-338-19325-1

10 9 8 7 6 5 4 3 2 1   18 19 20 21 22

Book design by Abby Dening

First edition, September 2018

Printed in the U.S.A.   23

Scholastic US: 557 Broadway · New York, NY 10012
Scholastic Canada: 604 King Street West · Toronto, ON M5V 1E1
Scholastic New Zealand Limited: Private Bag 94407 · Greenmount, Manukau 2141
Scholastic UK Ltd.: Euston House · 24 Eversholt Street · London NW1 1DB

To those kids who are decoding the past and creating the future

PART 1

Molly

Molly was tired of fighting for her life. She wanted to curl up someplace cozy and sleep for a week.

The blue forest she was hiking through looked safe enough, but she no longer believed in safety. She didn't think she'd ever feel safe again.

The trees around them, for one thing, didn't look exactly like trees, more like blue broccoli or cauliflower. And she knew that none of the small creatures rustling in the toothy bushes would look much like the animals she was used to.

She said out loud, "At least for once there's a path."

"Does that make you feel better or worse?" asked Hank, the tall, unhappy-looking boy at her side. "That means someone made the path."

"Or some*thing*," said Anna, the third and final person in their scouting party. She was walking a few steps behind them, looking around carefully at the overhanging cauliflower. "Maybe the path we're on is like a deer path," she mused. "Some animal goes back and forth to the water this way."

"It's a wide path," Molly said. "It would have to be a . . ." She didn't finish the sentence.

"Pretty big deer?" Anna finished. "Yes. Larger than almost any animal on Earth."

"Let's not think about it," said Molly, shaking her head. She was supposed to be the leader of the group. She couldn't let herself be frightened.

"In any ecosystem," Anna explained relentlessly, "there is always an apex predator—a predator at the top of the food chain who is too big to be killed by the other animals. Usually some kind of hypercarnivore."

Hank muttered, "Oh, that's swell."

Anna had a way of reminding people of facts they didn't really want to remember. She believed a little too much in always telling the truth.

Molly argued hopefully, "Or maybe this path was made by some big plant eater. Like an elephant."

"Yup," said Anna. "That would be good, but there would still be an apex predator that would eat the giant herbivore— and it would probably be bigger and meaner."

"All right," said Hank. "We get the idea."

"Or," Anna continued, "something smaller but more deadly—a vicious pack animal, a super parasite, a . . ."

"We'd better keep quiet, then," said Molly. "We don't want to attract attention."

Sometimes, with Anna, it wasn't worth trying to paint a happier picture.

This constant sense of danger was what really exhausted Molly. For more than a week, there had been no rest. Birds with beaks as sharp as knives, sand that ate people whole, vines that dragged struggling animals to their doom, weird tech that threw people forward in time or hurled kids into the air . . . She could barely remember the last time she had relaxed. Every moment, she and the others had to watch out to make sure no new beast was stalking them and no new peril was about to swallow them whole. She was an optimistic person, but sometimes the constant watchfulness made her bone-weary. Ten days ago, Molly, Anna, and their whole Robotics Club had been on an airplane jetting off to Tokyo, where their toaster-size Killbots were going to compete in a mechanized soccer match. Then, somewhere over the Arctic, their plane had mysteriously come under attack. The top of the plane had been torn right off and a strange electrical force had buzzed through the cabin, plucking at each passenger as if choosing chocolates from a quality assortment, hurling out the ones it didn't want—just before the airliner crashed.

When the group of kids had stepped out of the wreckage, they found themselves not in the middle of the snowy wastes of the frigid pole—but in a tropical jungle. Since then, they'd been trying to escape through jungle, desert, and forest. And each setting they passed through claimed lives.

A few days after the crash, Anna and some of the others had stumbled on some kind of a map: an interactive model floating in a cave. It showed a whole miniature world nestled in a tear in the earth, a rift. At the one end was the jungle where their plane had crashed. At the other end was a weird structure bristling with needle-sharp spires—some kind of city, maybe, or a futuristic castle jutting out of the rock. That was their goal. That was where they'd find answers.

And, hopefully, help to get home. Molly was particularly anxious to find some adults who knew what was going on and might provide medical attention. She'd been bitten by a monster bird and had been infected somehow. Her body was corrupted. She was changing. No one else knew how bad it had gotten.

Molly reminded herself: The important thing, in the midst of all this confusion, chaos, and horror, was to keep focused on short-term goals. For the moment, the three of them were just on a scouting mission. They were supposed to find the huge lake or miniature sea they'd spotted from a distance a couple of days before. The next step of their voyage would have to be across that sea if they were going to reach the city of spires.

But while they'd been thrashing around in the blue cauliflower forest searching for the shore, they'd come across this path. It was wide and beaten down. On the one hand, it was a huge relief to walk easily without kicking their way through alien bushes all the time and hopping over fallen stalks. On the other hand, they might run into whatever monster used this route.

"We used to hear something big in the forest near our compound sometimes," said Hank. "It's probably what made this." Hank wasn't originally with Molly's team. He'd lived in this strange world for a long time—longer than he realized—setting up a defensive camp with the members of his stranded marching band. "Whether it's a plant eater or a meat eater, it killed a couple of us."

"And we heard it on the other side of this biome," said Anna. "When we came into the blue forest. It must be huge."

"Okay," Molly demanded, "let's talk about trees instead. Anna, you know a lot about life science. Have you ever seen pictures of trees like this anywhere in the world?"

Anna craned her neck, peering around them. "No. They look less like trees and more like cruciferous vegetables. For example, the leaves don't look like deciduous tree leaves, more like broccoli florets. Maybe they're some kind of prehistoric tree . . ."

"Or," said Molly thoughtfully, "a tree from the far future."

"We didn't have trees like this in the forest where we crashed," said Hank. "Or weird pods like that." He pointed into the upper story of growth. Huge plant pods hung from the upper branches.

"We're in another biome," said Anna.

"I don't know what that means," said Hank.

"A biome is a community of plants and animals that—"

"And I actually don't care," said Hank.

Anna fell silent, looking bruised.

Hank was still peering up into the trees at a pod that had split partway open. "It looks like there are seeds inside. Like peas. They're huge . . . I wonder if we could eat them." He looked around, kicking the underbrush, shoving branches back. "Looking for a stick," he muttered.

"Here's one," said Anna, trying to be helpful.

"Thanks." Hank took it and started waving it over his head, as if trying to bash a piñata.

Wham! He hit the pod, and it started swinging, splitting wider. *Wham!* He hit it again.

Then a volley of shots rang out. Explosions.

Molly screeched—she'd been hit in the cheek.

She dropped to the ground. "Get down!"

The others crouched. Their hearts pounded. But the forest had gone silent.

As they looked for their attackers, they noticed they were covered in goo.

Molly reached up and grabbed at the dart that had hit her. She pulled it out.

It wasn't a dart; it was made of wood, but not carved.

"What is that?" whispered Hank.

Molly held it up for the others to see. "Theories?" she said.

Anna was squinting up at the shell of the pod that still rocked back and forth over their heads. "I think," she said, "it's a seed. From an explosive vegetable."

"Huh?" Hank straightened up.

"It's a fruit or vegetable that spreads its seeds with some kind of little detonation when they drop to the ground. So they'll travel beyond the range of the parent plant. Like other seeds spread themselves by attaching to animals' fur or passing through animals' digestive tracts." Anna pointed. The little firecracker detonations had spread globby plant flesh and seeds all over the path. A few of them stuck point-first into the ground. One of them had shot straight into Molly's cheek.

"I wonder if the plant flesh is edible," said Anna. "There's a lot of it."

"Yeah," said Molly. "Some went into my mouth when I screamed." Hank and Anna looked at her in horror. She admitted, "It was delicious."

She knew, however, that her body was no longer digesting things exactly like a human. She didn't want to tell them how alien she felt sometimes, since she'd been bitten. Maybe the red flesh of the exploding vegetable was only safe for her, and for Cal, who was undergoing the same transformation.

"We can take some back," said Hank. "We'll try it tonight in controlled conditions." He shoved some of the gooey rind into his bag.

"Javi will want to name it," said Molly, always thinking of her best friend.

Anna suggested, "Maybe pea-splosion?"

The other two looked at her.

"Not good?" she said.

"Sounds like you waited too long for the restroom," said Hank.

"Ohhhh . . ." Anna said.

For a time, all three of them tried to think of punny names for detonating fruit. Bam-anas. Blew-up-berries. They were almost like normal kids, making up normal, stupid jokes.

And in that moment of silence, Molly perked up. "Hear what I hear?" she said. "Waves on a beach."

She held up a finger and they all listened closely.

"I think we found our ocean!" she said.

They jogged forward.

As they crested the next hill, they saw the rift's sea. It was a dark green plain of chilly water, troubled by winds, with whitecaps lashing against the rocky shore. It stretched farther than the eye could see.

The pebble beach was broken with several outcroppings of boulders. Shredder birds circled above them, crying forlornly.

"I can't see the other shore," said Hank, squinting.

"The human eye can see about three miles at sea level," said Anna.

"Because of the curvature of the Earth," Molly said, nodding. She walked backward up the slope. "There's the far side. Now I can see it. So maybe the mini-sea is five or six miles across? Take a look and—"

A boulder outcropping had moved. At first, Molly thought it was a trick of her eyes. She blinked and looked again.

No question. A heap of boulders shifted. Slanted. Stood.

Molly shouted to the other two down on the beach, "This way! Watch out!"

Now Anna and Hank saw the motion. They stumbled backward on the loose gravel as a giant body rose from the beach.

It was not really boulders. It was alive. Something had been digging.

At first, Molly couldn't make out its shape. She just saw muscle and hide and glinting metal. It heaved out of the pit it had dug.

And it started to stalk toward them.

2

Anna

It was like nothing Anna had ever seen—no head visible, just a burly, armored trunk on top of muscled animal haunches, powerful arms cocked back like a praying mantis's front legs, ready to grab. The thing was easily twenty feet tall.

She and Hank staggered away as it surveyed them from its height. Molly was yelling something at them from up on top of the rise, and they ran toward her.

The creature stirred itself and stomped up the beach. Only a few steps and it was right behind them. Another step and it would crush them.

Hank grabbed Anna's hand and pulled her to the side. She tripped and spun, but he held tight, and she was still standing when a huge clawed foot smacked into the gravel beside her, right where she had been just a second earlier.

Hank shoved her into the underbrush.

They thrust vines and bushes out of their way, crashing on all fours away from the beach. Anna had no idea where Molly was.

Anna felt something clutch her. She swiveled her head and saw branches snagging at her shoes. The beast was sweeping an arm side to side through the underbrush, searching. Hank yelped and threw himself forward. The two kids clambered through bushes that scratched and tore. The crash of vegetation followed close behind them.

And then stopped.

Anna became very aware of the silence. She and Hank suddenly sounded loud in the quiet morning. She reached out and snagged one of his belt loops. That brought him to a halt.

The thing was standing up straight now. It truly had no head. It was waiting, for some reason—biding its time.

Anna hardly dared to breathe.

Surely it saw them.

She couldn't tell if it was a robot or some gigantic animal. *I wonder if it's a combination*, she thought rapidly. *Some kind of cyborg. It would be interesting to investigate the interface between living muscles and the mechanized—*

There was a crash—a series of crashes—off to the side. Molly's footfalls as she fled.

Hank's mouth dropped open. How could Molly be so stupid as to draw the thing toward her? Just to save them?

Another footfall.

Abruptly, the thing leaped. Its arm flew out and punched into the forest.

"Molly!" Anna screamed, unable to keep silent.

3

Yoshi

I should have gone with the scouting party, instead of that idiot Hank," said Yoshi, sawing at a broccoli branch with his knife.

Smirking, Kira said, "You're just worried he's better looking than you." She handed the branch to her sister, Akiko.

"That's not it," grunted Yoshi. "He's a liar. He can't be trusted."

"But he's so tall," Kira sighed playfully. "Is that what's bothering you?"

Yoshi scowled. "He trapped his whole marching band in a time bubble."

"Girls love a boy who can slow down time."

"Would you stop it? I'm serious. We shouldn't have even let him come along on our march toward the city of spires. We should have left him back in his base camp. No one trusts him. And Molly shouldn't have taken him along to look for the route to the sea."

refully, "I think Molly chose him specifically
usts him. She wants to give him a chance to

y of things to say to that, but all of them
...u whenever Yoshi had too much to say, he said
nothing.

Kira said, "Hank has to get used to someone else being in charge."

Yoshi frowned. There were times that he wished he could leave this group of amateurs behind and go off on his own, or that he, instead of a faceless electrical force from beyond, had been allowed to make a few key decisions about who would be stuck in this rift.

His father had taught him to be a decision maker, grooming him for the boardrooms and glass-walled offices of Tokyo and New York. "First, name the problem. Second, think through all the tools at your disposal. People often forget that a knife is also a mirror, and that an enemy is often more useful than a friend. Third, think through the pros and cons of each solution. Then decide. But once you've chosen, don't look back. The decision's over. It's in the past. It can't be changed. There's a new decision to be made."

His father couldn't have offered better advice for living in this weird alien landscape, Yoshi realized sourly. In a sense, he now spent his days living by his father's philosophy: naming problems, quickly picking solutions, dealing with the sometimes bloody aftermath. *Did you do anything useful today, son?* his father would ask.

Fed a whole group of starving kids in the wilderness, would be his defiant answer for today, and he hated that it still didn't feel like enough.

Of course, when Yoshi had quite literally chosen his tools in the past year, he'd made a bad decision: He had stolen a priceless katana, four hundred years old and forged in feudal Japan. If he ever got back to civilization, the fact that the katana had kept him alive when he was confronted by tangle-vines and razor-beaked shredder birds wouldn't protect him from the legal consequences of smuggling a priceless blade out of the country.

Yoshi, Akiko, and Kira were building a trap to catch slide-whistle birds, using the webbing they'd pulled from the plane as a net and the pliable broccoli tree branches as springs. Akiko would use her flute to attract the birds, and then, when the birds had settled, Yoshi would snap the trap closed. It would be a lot easier than throwing the net into the air each time and hoping they caught something.

Yoshi saw that on the other side of the clearing, three more kids—Javi, Kimberly, and Crash—had returned with wood for the campfire. They were talking loudly in English. They didn't understand the Japanese that Yoshi spoke with sisters Akiko and Kira. Two of the kids, Kimberly and Crash, were from the past, from a time when people still danced the Twist and the Mashed Potato. They didn't just speak English—they spoke in the English of the mid-twentieth century.

"Golly!" Kimberly cried, throwing down her load of sticks.

Yoshi smiled to himself.

"What's funny?" asked Kira. She and Akiko spoke almost no English.

"Kimberly uses words no one in America has used for a long time," Yoshi explained. "Seeing her is like seeing my grandmother as a girl."

Now serious, Kira said, "I'd never forgive Hank if I'd been in that camp and he'd pushed me into the future without telling me. When they get home—if we all get home—their parents will be old or dead. All their friends will have grandchildren."

Akiko shook her head, as if she could frighten off thoughts like gnats. "I don't want to think about it."

"About what?" asked Kira.

"What it would be like to discover our parents were suddenly ninety years old."

Kira, who was a bit of a troublemaker, joked, "At least then maybe Mom would have less energy. She'd spend less time flying all over the world and more time with us. It's hard to fly when you need a walker to get around."

Akiko pouted. "Mom would find a way."

Yoshi pointed out, "Air Pacifica puts you in your own little sleep capsule when you fly first class. You have everything you need right there. It's . . ." He trailed off.

Then they were all thinking about their plane crash, and all the people who had disappeared and were probably dead. The three stopped talking entirely.

They wove the springy branches through the webbing. Kira, who was in charge of the design, tied the flexible boughs to a frame.

"Almost done," she said. "Those cute little birds won't have a chance."

Akiko frowned. "Don't say that."

"Why do you care if we kill a few slide-whistle birds?" Yoshi asked her. "The strong have to eat to live."

Akiko looked at him angrily. "Because they have the right to live, too. They just come over to us and listen to me play the flute because they like music. Then we kill them. And who knows what's waiting out there to eat us, thinking just the same thing you are?"

"I'm a predator," said Yoshi, "and I don't intend to become prey."

The trap snapped shut.

"Works!" said Kira. "Now to try it with real birds!"

She and Yoshi stared expectantly at Akiko, who glumly held her flute on her lap. They waited for her to play and attract the birds toward the trap. Akiko stuck out her tongue. Kira stuck her tongue out back. Miserably, Akiko put the flute to her lips and started to play a tune.

A serpentine voice in the bushes hissed, in English, "We all listen. But you don't even know what you're saying."

The three kids jumped and Yoshi reached for his sword.

Lying in the bushes was Cal, a clarinetist who was losing his humanity. His skin was glistening, shot through with scabs of yellow and green, growing spikes. His head was turned toward the dirt, but one eye glowered up at them, wet and red.

Now that he had their attention, he said, "Maintenance is in damage mode."

"He always says that," Kira complained, and mimicked in nonsense Japanese, *"Maitta ne Suisu iinda Meiji mode,"* which meant nothing really, but kind of, "We give up because things were so much better in Switzerland during the Meiji era."

Yoshi grinned.

Akiko protested, "He can't help it. He's sick." But she was smiling, and she whispered, trying out the words, *"Maitta ne Suisu iinda Meiji mode.* It really sounds like he's saying that!"

Kira wailed more dramatically, "We give up! Things were so much better in Switzerland!"

"That's not what it means in English," said Yoshi. "It's not about Switzerland."

"Then what's it about?" asked Kira.

"It means . . . 'The way of fixing things needs to be fixed.'"

Kira and Akiko stared at him.

"That doesn't make any more sense," said Kira. "We're going to pretend he's talking about Switzerland."

Akiko nodded. "I miss Switzerland."

From over by the unlit bonfire came the thwack and crackle of dropped firewood and a loud "OUCH!" Crash had dropped some sticks on Javi by accident.

"Forget it," said Yoshi. "The birds will never come near with that racket. Let's move away from the clearing."

Kira muttered, "No wonder the Americans call him 'Crash.'"

Kira and Yoshi picked up the trap, and Akiko followed miserably with her flute.

They walked down a hill and set up their trap at the base of it. Akiko began playing a lonely, lost tune. It wavered on the air, speaking of time passing and of friends who had disappeared. Kira's face grew serious as she listened to her sister play. Yoshi didn't like this sort of music—it was too soft for him, too sad. Why would anyone want to listen to something that made them weak and unhappy? He sat motionless, reminding himself that only the slide-whistle birds had to like the music. It was the last thing those little birds would hear before they became a barbecue dinner.

As Akiko played, however, the song got slower and slower . . . and now there were gaps between notes . . . like she'd forgotten what she was doing . . .

Yoshi glanced at her and saw her face wide with panic. She was hardly blowing into the flute anymore. It drifted away from her lips.

Something was behind him.

Yoshi spun, ready to attack.

At first, he only saw vines and creepers. Then his eyes started to pick out a giant shape, just as Akiko's had a moment before.

Between the blue trunks of trees, there was a dark form: wood. Carved wood. A towering statue.

It must have been carved from a single, huge tree—a kind that no longer grew in the blue forest.

Rising out of the forest floor was a mammoth statue of an alien figure—legs cocked backward like an animal's, giant muscled arms raised high in triumph, a huge barrel chest—and no head whatsoever. The carving looked ancient, riven with cracks and wormholes, tangled in alien kudzu, as if the figure fought against the forest itself, which sought to drag it down.

"Whoa," said Yoshi. "What is that?"

"And who carved it?" asked Kira.

And Akiko, shuddering, said, "Or *what*?"

Javi

But what *is* it?" said Javi, staring up at the wooden statue.

Javi, the two sisters, Kimberly, and Crash had just spent fifteen minutes trying to pull underbrush away from the thing so they could get a clear look at it.

"The head's missing," said Kimberly. "Too bad!"

"Do you really want to see a head?" asked Javi. "It's ugly enough as it is."

"Why, sure!" said Kimberly. "If there was a face, then maybe we could tell who made it. It looks like some kind of primitive idol. Like those ones they have in tiki lounges."

Javi shot her a look. "I don't know what a tiki lounge is," he said. "And maybe don't explain."

"Who do you think made it?" said Crash.

"If they looked anything like *it* looks," Javi pointed out, "they're not human. Look at those legs. They bend backward, like a lion's or something. Big claws. And those arms . . .

They're too rotted, but it doesn't look like they ever had hands."

Kira stood by his side, quietly drawing the statue in her sketchbook.

"Finally," said Javi. "Some real art for you to copy." He knew she couldn't understand, but she could tell he meant well, and she gave him a nice smile. He liked it when she smiled at him. Kira didn't smile often.

"See down near the feet?" said Javi, pointing. "I think those are carvings of the mites, the little robots we keep seeing. The wood's pretty broken up and mossy, but see what I mean? Sort of flat and boxy, with lots of legs?"

Kira stopped drawing and walked over to look where he was pointing. She got what he was saying, and said something in Japanese. He didn't understand. She flipped back several pages in her sketchbook. Kira tapped her pencil against the page. There was a drawing of one of the little robots they'd seen in the desert, just before Oliver had . . . well, disappeared. Under the sand. Forever.

"Exactly," said Javi.

"This is just wacky," said Kimberly. "Spooky. Someone must have carved this a long time ago."

"It's an amazing find," Javi agreed. "Better than our firewood."

Kimberly scrunched up her lips. "Those blue broccoli logs won't burn, will they?"

Javi shook his head. "Don't think so. They're kind of weird and spongy."

"This statue changes everything," said Javi. "Wherever we are, it once had art. It had a civilization. We're not on an alien planet—we know that because . . . well, this dude Caleb died to see the stars, and he told us they're the stars you see from Earth."

"So maybe we're still on Earth," Kimberly said, "but maybe our group from Bear Claw isn't the only one that traveled forward in time. Maybe you traveled forward in time, too."

Javi felt a creeping in his scalp. He realized how much sense Kimberly was making.

She continued. "And maybe everything we know about the Earth has changed. And there are new species and all."

Javi nodded slowly. "Maybe they've evolved in the centuries since we were born."

Kimberly pointed up at the idol. "And this is from some ancient civilization that still wouldn't exist for hundreds of thousands of years from the time when we were kids. Maybe we're that far in the future."

Javi felt millennia of time weighing down on him. Perhaps all of human civilization had fallen, or humans had evolved to the point where they were unrecognizable. Maybe there was no human world to return to.

Javi slumped against a tree.

"Dude," he said. "This is some bad news."

Yoshi, who was standing guard at the top of the hill, called down to them, "If you could all stop crying about history for a second, you might ask yourself the really important question."

Javi waited, a little annoyed. "Okay?" he said.

"*Are any of the things that carved that still alive?*" Yoshi said grimly. "Because *they* might be what we're headed right toward. Not anything that helps us. Just a city full of those, waiting to see what we do."

"Jeez," said Kimberly, looking up at the statue. "I hope that's not true. But maybe this is just a made-up monster, like the griffins or gargoyles on old palaces."

"I never want to find out," said Javi, backing away from the crumbling giant. "I hope none of us ever runs into this thing in the flesh."

5

Molly

Molly watched the towering beast stomp toward Hank and Anna. She saw Hank pull Anna into the bushes. The giant swept its arm back and forth through the underbrush. From where she crouched, Molly could see that it didn't have hands, just metallic attachments with rotating spikes.

Despite her panic, she had a robotics hunch: Those attachments had been made for digging and drilling.

But that wouldn't stop them from grinding up her friends into bloody hamburger clumped with strips of torn nylon.

Molly reached down and grabbed a fistful of rocks. She flung them along the beach, hoping to attract the cyborg's attention.

It was making so much noise that it didn't even notice.

Molly ducked into the forest and tried to triangulate, running in the direction Anna and Hank had crawled. She worked her way toward them. She would at least stand by their side as they confronted the monster.

But then everything went silent.

Molly froze, too. The monster must be listening for them.

Molly's own breath sounded loud in her ears. It seemed impossible that she couldn't be heard.

The monster was towering in the forest, about fifty feet away. Her friends must be just a few feet in front of it, crouched below. Somehow she had to attract its attention away from them—without showing where she herself was hidden.

Then she looked up and saw the pods. The pea-splosion pods. Most of them were sealed tight, not yet ripe. But one, just a bit up the hill, was split. It looked ready to drop its seeds.

Carefully, Molly reached down and picked up a rock.

She was not a great pitcher, but she hurled the stone through the jungle and hit the pod. She was shocked at the strength of her throw. It seemed almost unnatural.

The pod swung, struck.

The towering creature twitched. It must have noticed the motion.

And then the seeds dropped. There was a series of loud, brushy smacks as glob after glob exploded, hurling seeds.

The cyborg sprang to life. Between blue broccoli stalks, Molly caught glimpses of it stomping through the woods. It was charging away from them, up the hill. Then it stopped.

Clearly, it figured out what had made the noise. The cyborg stood motionless beneath the swinging pod.

Molly thought grimly, *Waiting for a kiss under the mistletoe.* She stood as still as she could. She had to get this patrol back to camp with all three of them alive.

The cyborg was on the move again. It crashed unhurried through the woods. It pushed aside the yielding blue trunks of broccoli trees and the hanging pods, heading back down the slope toward the water.

After several moments, Molly scanned the forest, but the monster appeared to be gone. Everything was absolutely still. Even the birds had the good sense to keep quiet.

Then she saw a stalk quiver. She saw the red of Anna's shirt. Anna was snaking along through the undergrowth. Hank was behind her.

Carefully, Molly worked her way toward them.

"What was that?" Hank panted.

"I couldn't tell if it was monster or machine," said Molly. "Theories? Conjectures?"

"It was both," Anna said. "It looks like it combines biological and inorganic material. A cyborg."

"Looked to me like a roasted chicken from hell," Hank muttered, and Molly unexpectedly found herself smiling. It *had* kind of looked like a roasted chicken, though a roasted chicken made of half tech, bulging with muscle, and three stories tall.

"We have to be careful of the path," Molly said. "That monster must go back and forth to the other side of the blue forest biome."

"If we don't use the path," said Anna, "how are we going to find our way back to the others?"

"I'll walk next to it," Hank offered. "You two stay parallel to me, but under the trees, where you can hide easily."

"The canopy," said Anna.

"Yeah," Hank agreed wearily. "The canopy. My clothes will stick out less than yours. If I see the thing coming, I'll run away."

"Why did it stop looking for us, I wonder?" Molly mused. "It just kind of gave up. Why not keep searching for us? There's something we don't understand, some robotic logic."

Anna brightened. "Like how we didn't understand that the jawbugs were actually attacking the compound because Hank stole that time-distortion device."

"Hey!" protested Hank.

"Anna . . ." sighed Molly.

"It was just an example," said Anna.

But it was too late. Hank was angry. "Oh, shut up." With a glare, he stormed off into the forest.

"Wait!" hissed Molly. She wondered whether he still planned on following beside the path to guide them back. It had been nice of him to offer.

"Anna," she whispered, "I wish you would think about things sometimes before you say them."

"Well, I bet his friends in the Cub-Tones wish Hank had thought about things before he stole a device that caused fifty years to go by in a few months."

Molly frowned at her and went after Hank.

Even though Hank was angry, he'd kept to his word. He was risking being seen so that they could all navigate back to the others. *He really is trying to make up for his mistakes*, Molly thought. *If the others will just forgive him.*

She knew what it was like to make tough decisions as a leader. She knew what it was like to lose people.

For twenty minutes, they walked without talking.

Then they saw Hank waving his arms. He didn't want to yell, but he was mouthing, *Look at this!*

Molly couldn't see where he was pointing.

Suddenly, he darted away from the path and cut across the forest. Molly heard him scrambling down rocks.

She and Anna rushed to catch up. He was leaping down a steep hillside into a hollow.

They followed, wondering what he'd seen.

"People!" he called back softly. They saw him point up.

High in the trees were rickety houses.

Another community! They had found more people trapped in the rift.

Anna and Molly scrambled after Hank, lowering themselves down the rocky slope. They heard Hank push through the brush, and then gasp.

They followed.

The three of them stepped out into a hollow in the middle of a thicket of alien trees. And the trees, the rocks—everything was scored with tiny marks in neat rows. The marking of days. A thousand. Two thousand. More.

Their vision blurred at the desperate chronicle of lost time.

6

Javi

Javi roasted two slide-whistle birds on a stick over their fire. Akiko was glaring at him from the other side of the clearing. Both the birds had landed in the trap at the same time, like lovers meeting to listen together to a concert. Then it had snapped shut, and Yoshi had pulled them out and wrung their necks.

Javi had no problem cooking dead birds. They were delicious. But he had to admire Akiko for sticking to her principles. She'd seen probably a hundred slide-whistle birds—as well as other little birds and beasties—get slaughtered in the past ten days, and it still upset her.

"Keep up the outrage," he called out to her, giving her a thumbs-up.

She wouldn't understand what he was saying, but she understood the thumbs-up, and she turned away in shame for drawing the birds to their death.

"Glad we got the fire started," said Crash. "These blue broccolis are useless for kindling."

"They're younger, I think, than the more Earthlike trees," said Javi. "It seems almost like the forest developed in a couple of stages." He would have to ask Anna about it when she got back.

It was still a couple hours before dark. The heat from the fire boiled the air above it. Looking through the smoke and distortion, Javi could just make out the idol down the hill. It stood in shadow, arms stretched out as if breaking free of the vines.

In awe, he said to Crash, "Imagine what civilization made that."

Crash was uninterested. "I don't read the science-fiction funnies," he said. "I like to read about normal stuff, like people with paper routes." He shook his head. "Now I'm living in a science-fiction comic."

Javi got analytical. "So why is that statue made of wood, when the robots were made of metals and plastics . . . or something like them? And the stuff Yoshi and Anna found in the cave—the model of this place—that was made of some super-advanced floating stuff, if it was even physical at all, and not just a hologram." He grimaced. "So why is this statue made of plain old wood? And why is it out here, far away from the city of spires, with nothing around it?"

"Maybe there's an underground city here, too," said Crash. "Or maybe it's older than the city of spires, like a thousand years older, from when the builders were just living in huts."

"It wouldn't have lasted," said Javi. "It would rot."

"It sure looks pretty beat up."

A croaking voice demanded, "They've always been with us. We made them."

Javi jumped and turned.

Cal again. Cray-cray Cal.

"Hey, Cal, buddy," Crash said to his old friend. "How are you doing?"

Cal pointed down toward the idol. He said, "You don't remember? You don't remember it walking down Maple Street, Robert, walking down Main, walking through Bear Claw? And it's a parade. And we're all behind it."

"No, buddy," Crash said sadly. "No, we didn't see any headless monster in Bear Claw. All the monsters have been since we've been here."

Cal vigorously shook his head. "I remember."

"Look, Cal, pal. You got to know you're a little . . ." Crash tapped his head. He didn't know how to say it politely. "You're a little, uh, couple of aces short of a deck right now. On account of being sick."

"I remember," Cal insisted. "They were everywhere, back then."

"Why don't you sit down and take a load off? In case your fever goes up."

"Not fevered," said Cal. "I remember. Just remember our music."

"Kimberly," Crash called. "Could you help Cal sit down? And get him away from the fire? In case he gets excited."

Kimberly jogged over. "Say, Cal! What's happening?" She took Cal by the arm.

"He's remembering a monster like that parading with us back home."

"They built our cities," Cal said. "I remember."

"Naw," said Crash. "Bear Claw was mostly built by John Sorgenson's dad, and he definitely had a head." Crash explained to Javi, "John Sorgenson's pop had a construction firm."

Kimberly shot Crash an irritated look. She said, "Cal's confused, Crash, but don't you make fun."

"He's not just confused," said Javi softly. "He's recalling the memories of . . . whatever he's turning into."

They all stared at Cal, at the network of pulsing green veins and glittering, feathery, poisonous scurf that was breaking out on his face and arms.

Kimberly faced her old friend and looked into his eyes. "Is that what it is, Cal? Is that what you're remembering?"

Cal hid his face and started to cry. "I remember them marching."

"Then tell us more, Cal," Kimberly urged him. "Tell us everything you remember."

"It was at home. They were marching. All of us played music. Not with our normal instruments. We were flying from tower to tower."

Intensely, Kimberly said, "In Bear Claw, Cal? Do you remember this happening in Bear Claw, Oregon?"

Cal started shaking his head. He didn't stop. He kept shaking it, crazed, getting more and more violent. He swung his arms around and let loose a desperate, bleating scream.

Crash said, "Keep him away from the fire!" while Kimberly, with a gentle voice but a grip like iron, said, "Come on, Cal. Let's go over there. Let's go over there, Cal, and calm down."

He pulled and shrieked.

Javi handed Crash the stick with the two birds toasting on it and rushed to Kimberly's aid. Together, they walked Cal away while he struggled.

"Hey," said Crash. "Hey! Javi, you overcooked the birds!"

Javi wasn't paying attention. He and Kimberly were sitting on either side of Cal, with friendly hands on his shoulder and leg.

"He's mixing up memories," said Kimberly. "They're all jumbly. Earth and . . . whatever this place is. He's confusing them."

"Or," said Javi darkly, "we're in another dimension. Another version of Earth."

Kimberly shook her head. "You people are strange."

"I'm serious, Kimberly. Have you ever heard of other dimensions?"

"No. Are you gaga?"

"Think about it: Maybe our airplanes slipped sideways, not to another time, and not to another planet, but to the same planet, to the planet Earth—but in another reality. A reality where monsters like that march down Main Street and Maple in Bear Claw, Oregon, and wave to the crowds while the Cub-Tones play 'The Star-Spangled Banner.'"

Kimberly's mouth was open in an O.

"Not 'The Star-Spangled Banner,'" sniveled Cal. "The greeting. We did the greeting." He pulled up his knees to his face and hid his eyes behind his hands.

Javi was just about to ask what greeting he was talking about when the three scouts returned from their foray. Hank, Anna, and Molly were all jittery with excitement.

"Javi! Everyone!" said Molly. "We've found something amazing!"

7

Yoshi

The outpost was incredible. Yoshi stalked through the clearing first, surrounded by the hatch marks on the trees. He felt like he was inside a mind obsessed with counting. Counting up to what? Two or three thousand?

Molly, Hank, and Anna had led them here, leaving Akiko and Kira to watch Cal and keep the bonfire going. The group spread out through the grove.

Hank said, "There are huts built up in the trees. Tree houses. But they're ruined. All busted up."

Yoshi felt a twinge of irritation. He didn't want Hank telling him anything. Yoshi should have been the one to find this place. He didn't want anyone showing him around, talking to him like a tour guide.

"Theories?" said Molly. "Conjectures?"

Yoshi was also sick of Molly treating this like a class trip to the Museum of Natural History.

Javi pointed at one of the hatch marks on the tree. "Whatever carved these probably had five fingers. They're crossed out in groups of five. That seems like our counting system. So good chance this is human."

"Thank goodness something in this wacko place is human," said Kimberly.

"The tree houses look human, too," said Hank. "I mean, normal."

"Did you go up and check them out?" Yoshi asked.

"No way up," said Hank. "Whoever built the tree houses must have used a rope ladder or something that rotted later."

"No way up," said Yoshi scornfully. "What about the anti-gravity device?"

"Naaaw," said Javi. "Look at all the shredder birds in the treetops. Right now, they're just flying around. If we turn on the device, they'll all flock right here and cut us to pieces."

Yoshi shook his head. *No way up.* There was always a way up. You just had to be smart enough to step off the elevator and take the stairs. Or shimmy up the handrail.

"I'm going," he announced. "Give me the rope from the emergency kit." Anna pulled it out and handed it to him.

"It's way too high," Molly said. "The rope will never reach. And there aren't any branches close to the ground."

Yoshi walked around the base of the trees, looking up at the rotten wooden platforms high above. He went to the narrowest trunk and slung the rope around it. Then he began fastening the rope in a loose belt around himself and the trunk.

"I'm going to keep inspecting the area," said Javi, "so I'm not looking when you fall to your death."

Yoshi didn't think that deserved an answer. He kept tightening the rope, checking to see if it had enough give, enough play.

"There's not much daylight left," said Molly. "Why don't you do this tomorrow? We need to get back to the fire."

When Yoshi had looped himself to the tree, he put his foot carefully on a gnarl and pulled himself tight against the trunk. He clutched the bark fiercely with both feet and one hand; with the other, he flipped the rope belt he'd made upward. That gave him support to straighten his knees and go another couple inches higher. He repeated the process. Yoshi clutched at the sockets of broken branches. He was making slow progress.

"Whoa. Look at this!" Javi cried from the other side of the tree. "Obviously a sign this camp was made by humans!"

Yoshi wanted to know what Javi had found, but he figured anything up in the treetops would be cooler. No way was he turning back now. He kept up his slow ascent.

"What is it?" Anna asked Javi, down below.

"Some kind of machine."

"Duh. I can see that."

"But there's a name in English. 'Wannamaker.' I can't read the rest. It's all rusted."

"This is so weird."

Yoshi didn't care what stupid stuff they found on the ground. He kept on shimmying, heaving the rope, leaning back, and gripping.

Javi called, "Hey, Molly, come take a look at this machine! What do you think it was?"

"What does it look like?"

"Old-timey."

"The name is in English," Anna reported, "'Wannamaker.' But it's hexagonal. And it has some kind of keyboard. Inside, there are these little tubes . . . They look like valves . . ."

Javi called up to Yoshi, "Come down and take a look at this!"

Molly said, "Are you okay up there?"

Yoshi didn't think they needed an answer. If he wasn't okay, he'd be falling. He kept climbing.

"Wow," said Anna. "He really has strong thighs."

"Do you think it's an internal combustion engine?" Javi asked his fellow engineers.

From the other side of the grove, Hank called out, "And there's a stove over here!"

Kimberly added, "It's actually a grill, not a stove. A little metal grill."

"Looks old," said Hank.

"It's all orange," said Kimberly.

Voices were ringing out on all sides from below, trading information about their finds: pots and pans, rusted through. A few springs. Yoshi kept climbing. It felt good to be higher than all of them.

"That is so keen," said Crash, looking up at Yoshi's heels. "I want to do that. Can I do it next?"

Yoshi had reached the lowest branches. He hauled himself up and sat, panting. It was time to untie the loop that bound him loosely to the tree. Now he could work from branch to branch, a more traditional climb.

As he pulled himself up, he noticed that he was rising above the level of the blue broccoli trees and the weird pods. Made sense, he thought. The tree he climbed was more like a tree of Earth, and like Javi had said before, these trees seemed older and taller. They must have been a lot younger when someone built the tree houses in their branches. Yoshi wondered how long all of this had been sitting here in the forest, rotting.

He loved the feeling of exploration. One hand higher than the other. His feet lifting him toward the sky. This should have been how his dad trained him for excellence. Sending him out into the wild to conquer obstacles. This was how he really learned who he needed to be. For the first time in a long time, he felt good about himself. He was satisfied with his strength and his resourcefulness. He didn't feel like a half anything, the child of no nation. He felt whole.

He had reached the lowest tree house. There were three of them, all falling to pieces. One was almost entirely gone, just a hanging sketch of a hut made of wood. He pulled himself into a trapdoor and came to rest in the ruins.

Animals had built nests here over the decades. Birds flew by him, chittering with discomfort. Some kind of bubbly orb of flesh drifted past, twitching knobs in his direction as if sniffing at his sweat. An insect, maybe—a bug lifted by gas. It floated off through the treetops, bumbling down through the air to grace the tallest of the blue cauliflowers.

And in the other direction, Yoshi could see the sea.

It was gray in the dying light. It washed against the rocky beach. It was dotted with islands. Archipelagos. And miles away, in the expanse beyond it, another distant shore.

He could also see a cliff wall, much taller than the tree houses, which spilled water in thunderous falls down into the ocean.

Yoshi thought about calling down a report, but he could tell them soon enough. He drank in the height, the view, the distance, the knowledge.

Then he noticed something strange about the beach.

All along it, there were figures. They were standing at intervals, each one alone, each one motionless. They were barrel-chested creatures, armored, maybe three stories tall. Just like the one Molly had run into. Just like the one carved in wood.

But there was a whole row of them, a half mile or so between each.

And they guarded the ocean like sentinels.

Javi

I t's not just human," Javi said. "It's American."

They were looking at the pots, pans, and utensils they had dredged up out of the leaves. Though the metal was rusted and coated with ancient slime, the manufacturer's name could still be read on the handle of one fork, and it said, *Williston Co., Boston.*

The fork was the strangest thing Javi had seen since they'd crashed: to come across something so boring here, so American. Something which spoke of docks and brick houses and tablecloths and plates and fancy restaurants. Those things seemed more unreal now than howling monster birds or sand that ate children.

Tablecloths. Javi could hardly believe that there were actually still restaurants in the world: Somewhere, if people wanted food, they just walked into a place and said so, and someone brought it to them. And put it on a table with a piece of cloth on it so your dribbles didn't mess up the wood.

He thought of Thanksgiving with his family, the whole crowd yelling and passing stuff in crazy crisscrosses over the table, his uncles laughing, and his dad wearing a stupid apron. His mom bouncing one of her nieces on her hip, singing her a song.

It was another life.

Now here he was, in a world he didn't understand—a future or a past or an alternate Earth—a hallucination or lost kingdom or a horrible experiment played by sick freaking scientists. If it was scientists, he was going to pick up Yoshi's katana and hack them up himself.

But this fork told a strange story. It didn't look like a modern fork. Something about the size and proportion was wrong.

"Does anyone know about metal?" said Javi. He turned the fork over in his hand. "If there was an archaeologist here, they could tell us when this was made, based on what metal it's made out of. Like, stainless steel or whatever."

"It looks old-fashioned," said Molly. "Like my grandma's silverware."

Javi smiled. "Remember when you put one of her spoons down the garbage disposal? You ground it up really good."

Molly shuddered at the memory. When her mom was mad, she could be scarier than shredder birds.

"If that had happened to me," said Javi, "I would have used it as an excuse to never do the dishes again. 'Ma! It's not safe! Do you remember the time I ground up Grandma's spoon?'"

Molly inspected the fork. "Look at the way this is decorated. I bet it's from the nineteenth century."

"So it's been here more than a hundred years."

Molly nodded and shivered. "Maybe a lot more than that," she said. "We should head back to the bonfire. It's going to be night soon. And we shouldn't leave Akiko, Kira, and Cal alone for much longer. We've already been gone more than an hour."

"Hey, Yoshi!" Crash called. "You up there? You up there, Yosh?"

No sound. Javi moved a few steps to look up into the trees.

"Yeah," Yoshi called down. "I'm up here."

"Come on down," said Crash. "We're going back to the bonfire."

Another long silence. Then Yoshi said, "I'm staying up here tonight."

Javi yelled up, "Don't be an idiot, Yoshi."

"You're the ones down on the ground with the dreadful ducks of doom."

Javi rolled his eyes, but Molly said, "He's got a point."

She called up, "Okay, Yoshi. We'll be moving our camp here tomorrow morning. We'll see you then."

"Molly, that's just dumb," Javi said to her. "Leaving him alone up there overnight?"

She shrugged. "What can I do? It's Yoshi."

Hank said, "Is he always like this?"

"Like what?" Anna said protectively.

"Like Yoshi," Javi answered. "Yes."

"Let's go," said Molly, and they set off.

Javi was looking for another way to go up the steep slope. He shoved around a few bushes and grabbed at their trunks, pulling himself up. He wasn't as limber and strong as Yoshi, that was for sure. He wished they could use the stupid anti-gravity device without getting carved up by the local wildlife.

But then, in the bushes, he noticed something strange.

A prow. The front of a boat.

He scrambled around to the side.

"Hey!" he yelled to Molly. "Halt march. Check this!"

It was a rowboat. And it was almost rotted through, sitting on the hillside. It was surrounded by a lake of flowers.

And its passenger was dead.

A skeleton, still clothed in rotted threads, lay swamped in a pool of old leaves. Bright red blooms surrounded the gunwales, as if the skiff drifted gently on a vanished sea.

Javi's heart stopped. It was different, seeing a skeleton on TV and seeing one in real life. It had been a person, but now everything that remained just sat there like junk: rained on, snowed on, and blown by alien winds.

The skull grinned at him.

Someone, clearly, had not gotten away.

9

Molly

"That could be us," whispered Javi, sitting at Molly's side by the bonfire. "Ten years, fifteen years."

"Everyone's thinking it," whispered Molly. "Not really the time to say it."

From several feet away, Anna announced to the group, "That skeleton will be all of us soon." She added, "Eventually, we'll become part of the food web of the jungle."

Molly shook her head.

They sat silently, eating *omoshiroi*-berries and the charred flesh of overcooked slide-whistle birds. Everyone was glum.

Anna broke the silence, clearly unaware of the pall she had cast over the group. "The fact that he was from America in the nineteenth century means that the rift has been here for a while, and that people have been getting pulled here since then."

"Swell," said Hank miserably.

"Actually, this idea is very important," Anna pointed out. "That means this place isn't part of an experiment run by modern humans."

Molly hadn't thought of that. It was a good point. There was no group of mad scientists squirreled away in the city of spires, twisting knobs and following video feeds of their struggles. This was something much stranger.

"Unless," said Hank, "unless they just put those bones there for us to find. As props."

Molly could tell Hank was just grumpy Anna had thought of something he hadn't. He was used to leading.

"What?" said Javi. "Like the little plastic treasure and the sunken ship in a fish tank?"

"Exactly," said Hank, but no one believed him.

Despite the day's discoveries, Molly didn't feel anything was much clearer that night as she lay awake next to the warm battery they used to bolster the heat of the fire.

She wanted to check the progress of the weird change her body was undergoing. She could feel the rough poison-green hide spreading across her body, the thickening of cartilage in spikes and ribbons, all of it growing cancerous within her. Her body itched, as if covered with stiff scabs. She wanted to see what it looked like. But no one else could see. No one else could know.

She didn't want to end up like Cal. Even as she tried to sleep, she could hear him gibbering on the other side of the clearing. "Maintenance is in damage mode." And then Kira, waking from sleep, mimicking him irritably: *"Maitta ne Suisu iinda Meiji mode,"* whatever that meant.

Molly felt like she was holding her sanity together with both hands. She was supposed to be the group's leader. She didn't want to turn into a burden instead.

Physically, she felt good. Better even, than usual. She could tell she was getting stronger. She had noticed, in the encounter with the cyborg on the beach, that her reflexes were faster than they used to be. Her throwing arm, too. She never could have thrown that rock and burst open that pod before. She wasn't bad at baseball, but she wasn't *that* good.

That was almost superhuman.

No. *Clear your thoughts, Moll.*

None. Of. That.

She wouldn't collapse. She wouldn't turn into Cal, crazed with memories crashing into each other, skin iridescent as a bug's. Her hands were hers, her legs were hers, her mind was hers. They were Molly. She would never be anything else.

And she wouldn't end up a skeleton stranded in a sea of flowers.

She rolled closer to the warm battery that glowed beside her.

Comforted, certain of herself, she let her thoughts drift toward sleep.

She dreamed dreams of power: Flying. Clouds. The sun slanting through deep, rich, billowy clouds as she effortlessly soared past them, down into valleys, along riverways. Water glittered beneath her.

I'm always myself, she thought. *Those clouds are cumulonimbus.* She smiled. Even dreaming, she was a nerd. *Way up above me are cirrus.* She opened her arms and tumbled through the warm air.

The world is beautiful. The lakes shone gold in the sun. Other people flew by, happy the rains were over. The forests were in full bloom, a ruby red, *aka,* and as she fluttered over a mountain peak, she could see a row of agricultural cyborgs plowing the fields.

What?

Molly woke, her heart pounding. She sat up.

What was that? A dream? Or a memory?

She reached up to her neck to scratch an itch.

And that's when she discovered that the rough alien skin had encircled her throat completely.

10

Yoshi

The sea was beautiful at dawn. Yoshi knew because he'd been freezing all night in the tree house and had hardly slept a wink.

The cloudy layer that always filled the daytime sky caught the red from a sun somewhere. Yoshi sat on the platform, looking out over the blue froth of the woods all around him and toward the ocean under the pearly, roiling sky. The line of cyborgs stood motionless in the first light.

Yoshi figured one of the Killbot kids could probably tell him what kind of clouds those were.

He didn't really care. He just knew that it felt right to be sitting here, greeting the day alone.

His few minutes of sleep had been interrupted by the sound of someone letting out breath. He'd fumbled awake, ready for battle, only to discover that it was just another one of the gas-bag creatures, no larger than a soccer ball, drifting past on the morning breeze. It wriggled its stubby tentacles.

Now that Yoshi was awake, he spent some time sitting motionless with the katana in front of him. He concentrated on his breathing and on honoring his sword. It was the way a true warrior should start his day.

Having centered himself, Yoshi decided that this was the moment to explore the little set of huts, before the rest of the group appeared, shouting and making dumb jokes.

There wasn't much to explore up above. The tree houses had clearly once been connected by rickety bridges, but even these had rotted away, leaving only a few jutting planks. He swung from plank to plank, testing each one before he put his weight on it, being careful always to keep three points of solid contact on the tree at any time.

Anything that had been stored up here—blankets or clothes—had rotted or fallen.

It was time to inspect the grounds. Yoshi formed his loop of rope again, lashed himself loosely to the tree, and headed for the ground.

It was a lot easier going down than launching upward. Eventually, he decided, he could get really good at this.

He wanted to see the skeleton Javi had found. They'd all exclaimed over it, and they'd clearly thought he would be too frightened to sleep near it. He hadn't been frightened at all. Just cold, which was worse.

It lay in its rotten rowboat, half sunken in dried leaves.

Yoshi forced himself to start clearing the leaves from around the body. It made his skin crawl, but it was weak to be frightened by something that had been dead so long.

There's nothing left of the person, Yoshi reminded himself. He was not a believer in ghosts. He believed in the physical world.

He pulled out fistfuls of leaves and the stems of flowers that had wound their way in through rotten planking and around the ribs.

He was careful as he pulled out the leaves that bathed the skeleton. It would be important to find any clothing that might survive. The bones had long ago slid out of alignment, so the pelvis was somewhere near the knees. The arms had been spread when the person died. A belt buckle, festering with rust, lay somewhere near the spine.

And there, by the bones, lay a book.

Carefully, Yoshi lifted it. He knew books did not survive the passing years well. This one had been bound in leather, most of which dripped off as he lifted it. The cover was scarred with ancient decay. The pages were stiff with age.

With a slow spread of his fingers, he opened the book to somewhere in the middle, trying not to crack the spine. He peered between the brittle pages.

It was insane. The page was covered in frantic, tiny handwriting. The writing went in all directions. Every inch was filled with ink. He couldn't even figure out how he'd start to read it.

Every page was like that. Crammed with text, but almost unreadable.

Then, not too far off, Yoshi heard shouting.

The idiot circus was on its way. He couldn't believe they were capable of making so much noise.

No, wait—something was wrong. The pitch in the others' voices was rising. He dropped the book and ran toward the sound of their voices.

The group had been cornered by a gang of large feathered slugs.

Yoshi stopped running. "Really?" he said. "All that noise for feathered slugs?"

He was about to make fun of them some more when a slug leaped off a tree and tried to fold itself around Kira's arm. She was screeching at it—"*Get off!*"—in Japanese, and reaching for a stick to jab it with. It was almost as long as her arm and bunched itself, about to launch toward her head.

11

Molly

Kira grabbed a stick and whacked the slug. She peeled it back and it fell onto the ground, leaving her sleeve covered in clear slime.

The slugs, large as dogs, were mobbing the group now. Their feathered heads craned, smelling the air, as they slid off the slick trees. The group fell back, waiting for another slug to pounce.

"Once again," said Yoshi, "I have to save you idiots." He got into a fighting stance—*jodan no kamae*—and began swinging the katana in broad strokes, slicing the slugs neatly with each arc of the blade.

Molly felt embarrassed. He was right. When it came to fighting things, he really was the best of any of them.

Back, forward, left, and right he swung his sword.

The slugs kept coming, too stupid to realize they weren't going to win this one.

Akiko squealed Kira's name, pointing at her arm.

The slime was burning Kira's sleeve black.

"The slime is poison!" Javi shouted. "Quickly, Kira! Tear off your sleeve!"

"*Naifu!*" Kira demanded, and Molly realized she wanted the knife. Molly pulled it out and handed it to Kira, who quickly sliced around the seam of her sleeve. The fabric was rotting before their eyes. Her skin would be next.

She pulled off the sleeve and, using the tip of the knife, tossed it into the bushes.

Meanwhile, Yoshi had made short work of the other slugs. The last ones were slithering away.

"Good job," said Molly to Kira. Kira got the sense of what she was saying and smiled back.

Yoshi stared at Molly, wiping his blade. Molly could tell that he was waiting for *his* thanks. She didn't like his attitude—"Once again, I have to save you idiots"—but he had, in fact, saved them.

"Thanks, Yoshi," she said.

"Sure," he said, like it was nothing.

Molly thought to herself, *If he hadn't been here, would we have been okay? Or would we have been burned alive by the acid slime?* She decided they would have found a solution. They weren't as helpless as Yoshi wanted to believe.

"By the way," said Yoshi, wiping the last of the slime off his sword with some leaves, "I found a book. A diary. It may have information about who made the camp and how they got here." Molly disliked the way he seemed to be saying, *I just saved you. And I also found the best thing.*

But both of those facts were true.

The leaves he'd wiped his sword with turned black as if charred.

They all went to the clearing with the nineteenth century camp, where the trees were marked with the records of thousands of days spent trapped and alone.

Yoshi leaned down, picked up the old diary—and handed it right to Molly. "Check this out," he said.

Molly riffled through the pages as the others looked over her shoulders.

"It's a book written in four directions," said Javi.

"Someone was running out of paper," Hank guessed. "They tried to cram as much in as possible."

The writing filled the margins. On some pages, there were even lines written in between other lines.

"We need to read this," said Molly. "It may contain clues about where we are. And how to escape."

Hank snorted. "Clearly, whoever wrote it wasn't an expert at escaping." He pointed over at the skeleton in its skiff.

Molly kept going. "That's why we need to find a way to get across the sea."

"It's not a real sea," Anna said, somewhat unhelpfully. "Technically, it's an endorheic basin. Like the Caspian Sea."

Javi rolled his eyes.

"The basin, then," Molly said. "We have to find a way across the basin so we don't end up trapped here."

Hank shook his head. "We've got to stop just marching forward and ask where we're going and why. This is exactly why Pammy and the others stayed behind. We can't just keep pressing on without asking if we're going in the right direction."

Yoshi said, "Maybe *you* should have stayed back in your band camp, too."

Anna pointed out, "We know the city of spires is on the other side of the basin."

Hank shook his head. "I don't mean just whether we're headed the right way. I'm asking whether getting to the city of spires, as you call it, is actually the right goal."

"Oh, come on," growled Yoshi. "Let's stop wasting time."

"Stop fighting!" said Kimberly. "We just need to talk."

Hank frowned. "And anyway, we can't get across the ocean or basin or whatever you want to call it, because that"—he pointed at the rotten rowboat—"is the only boat we have. Plus, the shore is guarded by that cyborg that nearly killed us yesterday."

"More than one," said Yoshi. "There's a whole line of them."

"Really?" said Molly, wincing.

"Yeah," Yoshi confirmed. "One every half mile or so."

"Sentinels," said Anna, and Javi said, "Watchmen."

"For what?" Molly mused. "What are they guarding?"

Crash suggested, "Let's just turn on the low gravity and bounce past the cyborgs."

"No way," said Yoshi. "First of all, there are a lot of shredder birds around. They'll attack us when we turn on the low grav. Second of all, don't be an idiot. We can't jump toward the sea. We'll just get blown off somewhere and drown."

Molly thought it through. She crossed her arms and announced: "Here's what we should do. Split into two. A smaller group goes and observes the cyborgs. See if we can figure out why they're stationed there. What's their function? What's their logic? Come up with theories. Who wants to go do that? The rest of us stay here, seeing if we can learn anything from this guy's mistakes." She nodded to the skeleton sagging in the rowboat. "Someone will read the book—"

"Me," grunted Hank, just as Javi said, "I will."

They stared each other down.

"I found it," Yoshi pointed out.

Molly said, "Can you tell Kira and Akiko what we're talking about? They need to decide whether they'll go to the beach or stay here."

"No," said Yoshi. "I'm talking about something else right now. I want to read the book."

Anna said, "You are the worst translator."

"Because I'm not a translator. I'm the guy saving your butts."

Hank said, "We were doing fine saving our own butts before you ever got here."

"Were you? Because from where I was standing, it looked like you were lying to your little marching band while you all quivered behind—"

Kimberly insisted, "Could we please stop talking about people's butts?"

The argument left everyone angry. Hank, Crash, Kira, Akiko, and Anna headed off to watch the cyborgs from a distance. Javi and Yoshi, side by side, settled in to read the book. The rest poked around the site, looking for more rusted artifacts that might give clues as to where they'd ended up: on the Earth they knew or some other Earth with the same stars but its own history, its own species, and its own destiny.

12

Javi

The Whale Ship *LaRue, Outward Bound, June 15, 1885.*
At 11 AM sailed from the mouth of the river with a fair wind. Stowed the anchor cables & at 5 PM lost sight of the land and home sweet home. *We shall not see those streets and steeples until next summer.*

That was how the book written in four directions began. Most of each page was taken up with a straightforward journal of a whaling voyage in the Pacific Ocean, heading to the Arctic. It was written in large handwriting by Jacob Onslow, the first mate of a ship called the *LaRue.* The entries described the weather each day, what they'd done on the ship, and other ships they passed. *Wind blowing fresh. Took in sails, reefed main topsail & hove the ship to wind from westward at daylight . . . Passed the Tarquin Man-of-War, signaled and gammed.* Many of the terms were things Javi and Yoshi had never heard before. They had no idea what most of it meant. Neither one admitted it to the other. Occasionally, Onslow wrote down his latitude and longitude.

"Hey, that's cool," said Javi. "If we had a working GPS, we could actually chart the route of this ship from a hundred and fifty years ago day by day."

"If my phone worked," said Yoshi. "But if anyone's phone worked, we'd call 9-1-1 and get out of here."

Kimberly was walking by and overheard them. "What are you talking about?" she said.

Javi explained, "We could track this guy's trip on a map if our phones were working."

"You have maps in your phones?"

"Yeah," Javi said. "We push an icon on the screen, and it gives us directions on how to get home and stuff."

Kimberly laughed. "Our phones show us how to get home, too. We just follow the cord back to the plug." She shook her head. "That is wacko. You live in the future, you guys."

Yoshi muttered, "Not now, we don't."

Day after day of 1885 went by in the journal, and nothing interesting happened. Onslow wrote a lot about mizzens and topgallants and spars and tacking. There was almost nothing that sounded fun. Occasionally, he mentioned card games or shooting at seabirds or drunken darts played while the whole deck was swerving up and down on the waves. The trick of drunken darts was not to hit anyone in the mouth or eye. Sometimes a sailor named Muller played sentimental tunes on a concertina.

Yoshi was a slower reader than Javi, so when Javi reached the bottom of the page of the main text, his eyes would drift to the margins, where, scrawled in different directions, in tiny, cramped letters, much later entries were written, out of order. He'd go from boring stuff about all the day-to-day routine on a whaling ship to crabbed, broken phrases like fragments of a hallucination: *I have ascended to the heavens . . . Bertram is no longer human . . . Today the Colossus sang to us . . . Dear God, today we had to kill Bertram—he was become a devil. We fed him to the knife birds.*

Then back to the main text, and the dull story of whales spotted and chased, killed and cut up and boiled for oil.

"This whale blubber stuff is incredibly boring," said Yoshi.

"Believe me, it's going to get better," said Javi. "Let's skip ahead."

He flipped through pages, watching the latitudes rise. "They're heading north," he said. "Zero degrees latitude would be the equator. Ninety degrees north would be the North Pole. See, here . . . sixty-six degrees north and a bit. They've just crossed into the Arctic Circle."

The first day the crew of the *LaRue* passed into the far north, they killed sixty-three seals in one day on an island they discovered: a massacre. They skinned the corpses. They had to wash down the decks from all the blood. Perhaps this was the start of all their misfortune.

Their first week in the Arctic Ocean went well. They chased a slow pod of bowhead whales and picked them off one by one.

Then the winds died down entirely, and they were stalled. Onslow reported miserably that they were pressed up against the ice. The ship was locked in place. It could not move in any direction. The winter gathered all around them and settled in with its teeth. There was nothing to do but wait it out.

For the first month, they were fine, though trapped in place. They had plenty of meat. While snows fell all around them, Muller played them songs about the girls back home.

Filled with dread, Javi turned several pages—a month—and found that the crew was still stuck. Things had gotten much worse. Many were dead of hunger and frostbite. The cold was intense. Ice blocked the windows and frost grew on the walls. The men sat belowdecks, drinking and praying. They'd thrown the bodies of friends overboard. Onslow kept hoping for some kind of thaw. Instead, men kept on dying. The journal recorded their names.

When the ship could move again, there were hardly enough men to sail it: only eight left. The captain had died weeks before.

They drifted silently through a world of ice. Though they could take their bearings, they didn't know how to reach the open sea anymore. Onslow wrote, *I cannot believe anymore that somewhere there are still cities, and people, and opera houses, and carriages.*

One day, a storm descended. They could see nothing but white in the midst of the blizzard. *It is as if the hand of the Almighty has erased the world itself.*

When the storm passed, they found the ship moving swiftly down a wide corridor of ice, though their sails were furled. *God be praised*, wrote Jacob Onslow.

For two days, a strange current drew them on, as if they were being gently pushed toward salvation.

In the long Arctic nights, they thought they could see lights on the horizon in front of them. At first, Onslow assumed it was the aurora borealis, the glow that often swims through the frigid skies of the lonely north; but these lights held almost still, as if they were small moons. A mysterious current pulled the ship straight toward them.

The stars straight up above, however, were the stars he knew, and the familiar moon made its usual rounds. He found comfort in that.

He hoped that the silent current was leading them back to the open sea.

Though the Arctic nights were still long, there was often a glowing dome of cloud on the horizon in front of them, as if someone had their own private sun as well as moons. *For them*, Onslow wrote, *the polar nights would not be long in winter. The days in the land under those clouds last twelve hours. What Power could make day in the midst of Arctic night? I have faith that it is a Power that seeks to save us.*

Then they hit the waterfall. It was unimaginable. Screaming from the foredeck. There was a cliff. "The edge of the world! The bloody edge of the world!" The water was hurtling off of it. They were going to fly off the cliff into—Onslow couldn't believe it—what looked like a green forest far below.

There was no way, he knew, to save the ship. But he could at least jam it sideways for a few minutes—enough time, maybe, for them to lower a whaleboat and row for shore.

He brought them about; the ship slewed to the side, its railings bobbing and dangling above a three-thousand-foot drop. They hit boulders and the hull splintered. The force of the rapids made a thunderous roar.

Onslow shouted orders for them to lower one of the whaleboats. "Lower it on the lee side!"

Two of the men got into a whaleboat and they all worked the davits to get the boat settled beside the hull of the ship amid the roiling black waters. They prepared a rope for the rest of them to climb down.

The whaleboat touched the water, and the sailors on board gestured for them to lower the cabin boy down next. He was dangling over the edge, tied with a rope, about to climb down, when the ship heaved. It was cracking apart.

And at that, the whaleboat with the men aboard was sucked under the keel, into a whirlpool, and disappeared without even a shriek.

The cabin boy scrambled back on board the foundering ship. The six of them looked at each other in panic.

They ran to the starboard side, which hung out over the cliff. Onslow announced, "We're going to lower someone down who can push off from those rocks, and swing to the side."

The cabin boy already had the rope tied around him, but they realized he was too light to make a good pendulum. Mr. Wesley, one of the other men, held on to the rope, too, and the two were lowered gradually past the ship's hull, banging against the copper plating, then dangling out over a drop of thousands of feet.

Mr. Wesley told the cabin boy, "Don't worry. We're going to make it. We just have to kick and hold."

When they reached an outcropping, Mr. Wesley counted to three, and they kicked out with all their might. That started them swinging. As they passed the rocks in midstream, they kicked again. And again. Each time, they veered farther to the sides. Up above, Onslow and Muller swung the rope with what little force they could, and the pendulum swung wider and wider.

Finally, on each swing, they were shooting over rocky faces of the cliff, places they could cling.

"Now grab on to something!" Onslow shouted. *"This ship's not long going to hold!"*

That was easier said than done. The ledges flew by quickly. Wesley grabbed at the stone, but that just set the two of them spinning at the end of the rope. Views flashed by of forest— sea—jungle—snow—the crippled ship, leaning out over the precipice.

Finally, Wesley stuck out his heels and slammed hard enough into one of the ledges that he slowed them. The cabin boy grabbed a vine to steady their jerky swinging.

The boy thought it wouldn't be enough, that it would just tear off the rocks. To his surprise, he found that the vine pulled back.

The vine wrapped itself around his wrist and yanked. It pulled them to safety.

"Wonderful vine!" said Wesley. "Most excellent vine!"

They were standing on a ledge, three thousand feet above a tiny sea.

The vine seemed to really like the cabin boy. It wanted to drag him farther along the cliff. The cabin boy took out his herring knife and cut the frond off his wrist.

Wesley, meanwhile, tied the rope to a rock outcropping and signaled for the others to shimmy down. The next two—a sailor and the ship's carpenter, with his tools clutched to him—climbed down. Only Onslow and Muller were left.

Onslow, always a gentleman, suggested that Muller go first. Muller apologized and said he could not leave without his concertina. He bolted for the aft cabin. Onslow yelled for him to hurry. Once Muller had his musical instrument flapping on his back, he crawled down the rope, and Onslow, first mate now acting captain, officially abandoned ship.

The two men worked their way slowly across the roaring waters. From above came a hideous popping as planks and strakes snapped. Onslow roared that they should start sliding—never mind the rope burn!

But as they slid sideways, the ship's hull finally cracked to pieces. The bowsprit swung out over the drop and launched itself—masts tumbling, the whole thing yawing out impossibly from the rocks—soaring into the wet, tropical air.

The rope went slack as the ship fell. Muller yelped and dropped and would have been dashed to pieces hundreds of feet below if he hadn't been caught in the embrace of the tanglevine and held tight.

Onslow was not so lucky. As the others watched, horrified, he swung out over the abyss in the clear morning air, called out for one last time the name of his lady wife, and plunged with the wreckage of his ship into an alien sea.

"What?!?" Yoshi hollered.

Javi and Yoshi had been so wrapped up in the story of the shipwreck, they hadn't noticed that the last entry was not in Jacob Onslow's handwriting. It referred to Onslow as *he* instead of *I*. As they reached the end of that day's account, they saw that it, and the rest of the book, had been recorded by someone else entirely.

That day's entry was signed by name: *Sammy Cardosa, cabin boy.*

"Whoa," said Javi. "I didn't expect that."

"The Onslow guy just disappeared? That's it?"

"Wait one second," said Javi. "Let's think about the sun."

"That sounds incredibly boring," said Yoshi.

"No. Think about what Onslow wrote, about the glow in the clouds. It created a twelve-hour day. If we're near the North Pole, in the summer there's no night, and in the winter there's no day. But it seems like there's always twelve hours of daylight."

Yoshi was starting to catch on. "So the sunlight, as well as the moons', is artificial."

"Exactly. Something in this place is engineered to create daytime and nighttime, as if we were on the equator. Otherwise, think about it: Hank and the Cub-Tones would have noticed the days or nights disappearing. They would have figured out they were still near the North Pole."

Yoshi blew out a frustrated breath. "Nothing is real here."

"It's embarrassing that a nineteenth-century guy figured that out, but we didn't."

"On the other hand," Yoshi pointed out, "we're still alive."

The night of March 12, 1886, five survivors of the *LaRue* sat at the base of the cliff and shivered. The mysterious red moon rose above them. Muller's concertina had been slightly damaged in the fall and made a high whistle when he played it. But accompanied by that eerie whistle, he played a hymn to remember all the crew members they'd lost.

The next morning, at a time the real sun would never touch the Arctic, something lit the clouds—a fake sun—and they saw a misty forest just a mile away across the water. *It is a miracle. It looks like the Garden of Eden*, wrote Sammy Cardosa, cabin boy. *It was lost at the beginning of the world, but we found it here in the ice and snow.* That day, they gathered timbers from the bobbing remains of the ship at the base of the waterfall and bound them with dead tanglevine to make a raft.

They pushed off and paddled their way toward the forest. They could see birds circling in the air above red trees. Nearby, a whale sounded—or something the size of a whale, but covered in feathers. On the shore, they saw a huge statue.

"It's like the Colossus of Rhodes," said Muller. "The giant statue that stood over a harbor in ancient Greece."

"Or like the angel guarding Paradise," said Mr. Wesley, grimly.

They rowed toward it, hoping to meet the sculptors who made it.

Before noon, they had reached the shore. They pulled their raft up on the rocky beach. They didn't see anyone around the feet of the giant statue.

Javi could only imagine their horror as the statue started to move. It started to walk toward them, tall as a ship's mast. It raised its arms. The crew of the *LaRue* sprinted for the forest—all but Mr. Cressy, the ship's steward, who gawked at the armored monster and could not move.

Young Sammy saw the Colossus reach Mr. Cressy. The steward still did not run, but dropped to his knees before it. He stared up at the void where its head should be. It raised its massive, clawed foot. Bowing in front of the monstrosity, he pleaded for his life.

It crushed him utterly.

13

Anna

Anna was not happy to be stuck in a scouting party with Hank again, though she had to admit they had worked pretty well as a team the last time they confronted one of the cyborgs on the beach. But when Molly wasn't around, Hank got bossy.

"We can't walk on the giant path," he said. "That's where the cyborgs walk."

"Obviously," Anna muttered.

Crash said, "Great point, buddy!" Crash was always enthusiastic.

Akiko and Kira listened, but Anna guessed they probably couldn't understand much of what was being said. She wished she could speak Japanese.

Hank led them on a tramp through the blue broccoli forest. Anna still noticed that the older timber—the fallen logs— were trees more like the ones they'd encountered in the last biome, where Hank and the Cub-Tones had holed up in their compound. For some reason, a new kind of forest was replacing the older one. She wondered how much help it was getting.

Then a thought struck her.

She announced, "I think I know why the cyborgs are there on the beach."

"Can we not talk right now, girls?" whispered Hank. "We don't want them to hear us. Right?"

For a second, Anna was embarrassed—she really was trying to work on not saying things at the wrong time, and maybe she'd been stupid—but then she caught herself, and she was just angry. Hank himself had been talking loudly, after all. Maybe he was just a jerk.

Suddenly, Kira cautioned them with a wave. "*E! Nani kore?*" she hissed.

She was pointing at a glint through the trees.

Anna's stomach dropped. Metal.

Armor? A cyborg?

No. It wasn't moving. It was a pile of scrap.

They crept closer to it. Over the rattle and occasional crack of branches under their feet, they could hear the waves roll upon the stony beach.

There, where the forest met the rocky shore, was another graveyard of robots. They'd seen one like this in the forest near the Cub-Tones' compound—the site of a battle . . . or a massacre. The casings, limbs, and chassis of robot mites were jumbled in a heap. They were seared and melted. Some had been stomped on. Clearly, some of them had been there for a while: Small flowers grew out of the corpses lowest on the pile.

Down the beach, a couple hundred feet away, one of the guardian cyborgs looked out to sea.

Hank made finger movements to suggest that he and Crash would sneak one way around the pile to observe the beach, and "the girls" should go the other.

Anna beckoned Akiko and Kira, and they set off.

Their job was to gather data to figure out two problems: first, how to get by the cyborgs, and second, how to actually cross the basin without a boat. If the cyborgs weren't around, there would be time to build a raft and drag it down to the water. As it was, they'd hardly make it past the edge of the forest before they'd be hamburger.

As they crept around the pile, there was an awful stench. Decay. Anna gagged. It was rotten and fishy and sweet, far too sweet, all at once.

Then she saw that one of the corpses on the pile wasn't tech. She almost vomited.

It was a sea creature, about eight or nine feet long—a large white flank with tendrils. She couldn't even tell the shape anymore, because the beast had been crushed and left to rot. The flesh was drooling off shattered bones. A huge swarm of flies jumped and danced all over it.

Trying to hold their breaths, Anna and the sisters staggered past the rotting body.

They made sure they were well away from the smell before they crouched in the underbrush and took up their post watching the guardians.

There was something almost majestic in the long row of cyborgs, each posed on the beach, each surveying the ocean. A whole line of them reached away into the distance, until they faded in the silver morning mist.

"I wish you could understand English," said Anna, "because I really do think I know why they're there, and it kind of drives me crazy not to tell someone."

Kira could guess what was going on. She offered Anna her pad and pencil.

Anna tried to draw a diagram. She was terrible at drawing. The sisters looked at her stick-people pictures and shifted their mouths around. Anna kept drawing circles around trees. She added arrows and dotted lines. The page was a total mess. After a while, Kira, the real artist, couldn't help herself, and started to laugh.

Anna was irked. Then she looked down. Wow, she realized, she really *was* a terrible drawer—so she smiled, too, and for a moment, the morning was actually nice.

They sat together for what seemed like an hour. The cyborgs didn't budge. Maybe two hours. The three girls took turns dropping off to sleep. The sun was warm on their faces. Eventually, Akiko nudged Kira awake and nodded toward the shade at the edge of the forest. Anna suspected she was warning her sister that she was going to get a sunburn and be miserable.

"I burn, too," said Anna, to make conversation. "Once, on Cape Cod, my arms turned purple."

By the third hour, Kira was drawing a beautiful building in her sketchbook. It looked like an old mansion somewhere in the mountains.

"Where is that?" Anna asked.

Kira wrote, in French, *L'Académie*—which Anna assumed was their boarding school in Switzerland. Akiko was whispering about it with delight. She clearly loved the place.

"*Maitta ne Suisu iinda Meiji mode,*" said Kira, apparently a private joke between the sisters.

Anna didn't understand how anyone would choose to be at a school so far from their parents and from their homes, so far from everything known. Of course, there were a lot of things

Anna didn't understand about the things people did. But this was something she felt strongly: She never wanted to be away from home again. And not *just* because her first trip away from her parents had thrown her into a nightmarish landscape of killer birds and leaping scorpions.

Anna liked a comfortable routine. Usually, she needed it. Her parents understood that. They knew how to help her through the day. They supported her. When she was little, her parents had written out a daily schedule for her, so she wouldn't feel lost.

Though, on the other hand: Wow. She was doing pretty well, now that she thought about it. Here she was, climbing cliffs, fighting robots.

She wondered: When she got back to civilization—if she got back to civilization—would she be the same as she'd been when she left? Or would she be stronger and more heroic still?

Would she, for example, turn out to be the kind of person who could just text (for example) Yoshi, and—

Akiko said something in warning. There was action on the beach.

About a mile away, a cyborg giant was on the move. It stomped down toward the water.

The two sisters were whispering rapidly to each other. Akiko clambered up the pile of robot corpses to get a better view. Anna stood by her side, hoping they couldn't be seen by any of the other guardians.

Something was coming out of the sea. The giant walked to meet it.

At first, they could only see a movement in gray breaking the waves. Then, it became clearer—it must be several moving things. Several small robots. A swarm of mites.

The cyborg moved to stop them. The mites shot past it up the shore, and Anna found herself reminded of the cockroaches in her apartment at home. The cyborg stomped on several—and then began firing. There were brief flashes. Maybe the robot swarm was firing back. The cyborg tilted and stumbled, but remained standing. Other cyborgs left their positions and jogged toward it. The beach thundered.

The swarm scuttled around them. The blasts grew louder. One of the cyborgs was hit badly. It toppled.

"Let's go find Hank," Anna whispered. "If the cyborgs win, they're probably going to dump the bodies on the heap right next to us, with the rest of the dead robots."

The three crept back, past the stinky sea corpse and around to the other side of the pile.

Anna saw the boys crouched in the bushes before they saw her.

Crash was watching the battle of the robots as if it were a football game. He was making fake quiet stadium noises ("And the crowd goes wiiiiild . . . Yaaay . . .") and pumping his fists in the air.

Hank was just watching, but as he watched, he murmured. "Okay, Crash. Crash, calm down for a second. Answer my question. Just answer my question."

"Aw, neat-o!" said Crash. "This is amazing."

"Answer my question. The girls will be here soon."

At this, Anna stopped moving. What was he talking about that had to be kept so secret?

She put her fingers to her lips and the sisters stopped in their tracks behind her.

Crash said, "Yeah, sure, Hank, buddy. You know I'm always behind you. Drums follow the woodwinds, huh? Wherever they shall go?"

"So if there's a chance for me to take over the group, you'll stand with me, right? You agree Molly doesn't know what she's doing, right? I can count on you?"

"Of course, pal!" Crash slapped his friend on the arm.

That's when they saw the girls. Hank jumped in surprise, but Crash just smiled a big smile. "It's the chicks!" he exclaimed. "What did you think of the big game?"

14

Molly

Oh my gosh! What *is* it?" Kimberly gasped, looking at the object they'd just found in the bushes.

Molly sized it up. "I think it's a table made out of planks and giant monster ribs."

Kimberly put her hand in front of her mouth and laughed. "It looks like something from *The Flintstones*!"

"The what?"

"The show."

"I don't know what that is," said Molly, "but I would totally have this in my house."

"What do you think the bones are from?"

"They're too big to be a dreadful duck of doom." Molly shook her head. "Must be some other thing we haven't run across yet."

"Maybe a sea creature," Kimberly guessed. "They look like whale bones."

"Speaking of whale bones, I wonder how Javi and—"

Several explosions crackled through the woods.

Instantly, Kimberly and Molly went into defensive poses, ready to fight or run.

But the woods had gone silent.

Molly relaxed and ran her hand across her hair. "It's those stupid pods again. Another one must have fallen." Then a thought struck her. "Hey, let's go take a look. I wonder if there's a way to use their natural explosives to make . . . I don't know . . . bombs or something."

Molly and Kimberly climbed up the hill until they found where the fruits had just fallen and blown up. Spiky seeds, each one the size of a fist, were stuck into the ground all around the empty pod casing.

"How strong was the explosion when you got hit?" Kimberly asked.

"Not too strong. Not like a firework. More like a small fire-cracker. But it still stung. Let's try to look at one of the fruits before it explodes and figure out how it works."

They walked over to one of the hanging pods and looked up at it.

"Now," said Kimberly, "how do we get it down without it busting open?"

"Antigravity," said Molly. "We only need to use it for a second. The shredder birds won't have time to gather."

They worked out a plan. Kimberly stood under the pod, holding the antigravity device at the ready. Molly walked outside the effect radius. She picked up a stone and, with an arm that astonished her, hurled the rock at the pod's stem.

The pod split, dropping five fruits. Right then, Kimberly switched the antigravity on. The fruit drifted down sideways, landing as soft as bubbles on the forest floor.

As quickly as she could, Kimberly shut off the device. Already, Molly could hear the squawks of shredder birds attracted by the gravity bubble.

As the birds swung by up above, confused and disappointed, Molly and Kimberly ran over to the tumbled fruit.

Very gently, Molly picked one up. It looked like a large sphere with several big purple warts. When she held it against the light of the sky, she could faintly see the hard seeds clustered inside. "I've got a feeling it explodes when you pop these warts."

"That has got to be one of the worst sentences I've ever heard in my life."

"You know who'll want to pop the warts?"

"No one in the world?"

"Javi." Molly called down to the encampment, "Hey, Javi! Come on up here and check this out!"

When Javi and Yoshi jogged up, Molly showed them her find. "This is a fruit grenade," she explained. "Don't get too excited, Javi, but what I'm about to ask you to do combines zits and explosions."

"Great, Moll. Why did you think of me?"

Molly grinned at him. "I want you to poke a zit with a stick."

"I still want to know why you thought of me!" he squealed.

They set up their experiment, carrying one fruit grenade far enough away from the others that it wouldn't set off a chain reaction. Molly lay it down gently in the fallen leaves. Then Javi crept toward the grenade with a very long pointed stick, holding an old frying pan as a shield. "You can't be too careful with fireworks," he said. "I got a cousin who lost two fingers to a Screamin' Freedom."

He jabbed a wart with his stick.

The second the chemical in the wart mixed with the flesh of the fruit, the whole thing exploded with a bang. Seeds plinked against the frying pan.

"It's a two-part explosive," said Javi, looking down at the goo. "The explosion spreads the seeds, and it also keeps away animals who might eat the fruit otherwise."

"I bet the flesh of the fruit is nutrient rich," Molly guessed. "To help the seeds grow."

"Molly, it's organic gunpowder! Don't *eat* it!"

"Don't worry."

She didn't tell him why: Her gut knew already it would taste good. Her tongue tingled. She knew the flesh of the fruit would nourish her, especially the part of her that was not human. She got down and scraped some from a stone. Then, quickly—before Javi could stop her—Molly ate it. "It's great," she said. "Refreshing. Zippy."

Javi shook his head. "You are weird, girl."

Yoshi just glowered. "This is pointless. It's not explosive enough to hurt a cyborg, or even a person, unless you were really unlucky."

"There might be another use, though," said Kimberly.

"Especially if we could extract the combustive chemicals," said Javi. "We could make our own bombs. Stronger ones." He looked down. "Molly, stop eating that stuff. You don't know how it's going to affect you."

Molly looked up, embarrassed. Her mouth was smeared with red goo. It was delicious.

"Um," she said, "so what are you guys learning? From the book?"

"We're reading the main part of the journal first," said Javi. He told Molly a bit about the story of Onslow and Sammy Cardosa, about the good ship *LaRue* getting stuck in the

Arctic over the winter, and about the current that pulled it toward the rift.

"Have any conclusions?" asked Molly, standing up, trying to hide her interest in more red goo.

"I do," said Yoshi. "This isn't another dimension. This isn't another Earth. It's just like I said after I climbed up to that cave in the cliff wall. On the other side of the cliffs, it's the Arctic. Our own Arctic. Our planet. There's no mumbo jumbo."

Javi agreed. "The *LaRue* didn't go through a magical portal or anything. There were no UFOs, except the fake moons. There was nothing supernatural about it. The ship just fell down a waterfall."

Then they told Molly about the artificial sunlight, as well as the glimpses the crew of the *LaRue* had of the floating moons from a distance.

Yoshi said, "We just got to a part where they met a cyborg."

"They call it a Colossus," Javi added. "It killed someone."

"Any hints yet about how to deal with them?" Molly asked.

"Yeah," said Javi. "Don't get stepped on."

"Well," said Yoshi, looking scornfully at the grenade fruit, "*those* sure aren't going to help much with the cyborgs."

"The Colossuses," said Javi.

"Whatever."

"But the shells of the pods will help," said Kimberly. She had been staring thoughtfully at the empty husk.

"How?" said Yoshi.

Kimberly smiled. "I think we've found our boats."

15

Javi

For a week or so after the four remaining crewmembers of the *LaRue* landed on the strange rift continent, they lived in constant fear. Javi and Yoshi read Sammy Cardosa's descriptions of the sailors ducking into the woods, eating berries, and hiding from the Colossus, which waited on the beach. It took the survivors of the *LaRue* a full week to realize the giant offered no threat to them if they didn't approach the water.

They stayed in the forest. They encountered dreadful ducks. Luckily, one of the sailors, Mr. Scarlett, was a har-, pooner. He made a spear and kept the monster birds at bay.

The four of them crossed the alien woodland, noting weird species, until they reached the desert. Here, Sammy was caught up to his knees in the blood sand. When the rest pulled him out, they retreated back to firm ground. They watched a stupid elephant-pig wander out into the plain, drooling at the sight of some scabby plant. Immediately, it went down with a yelp.

They didn't attempt to cross the desert again.

It was at about this time that they found the hollow where they made their camp. Fewer dreadful ducks came to this part of the forest, and it was far enough away from the beach that they could only barely hear the heavy steps of the Colossus as it paced along the shore at night, keeping watch.

They built campfires. Every day Sammy cut a hatch mark in a tree to count the days they'd been there. Muller played songs and hymns for them all on his whiny concertina to remind them of home. They built huts to protect them at night.

Sammy and one of the other sailors clambered up the tall trees to act as lookouts. They were used to climbing up masts and ship's rigging. They sat in the high branches, surveying the forest.

From the treetops, they could see the headless Colossus and the ocean beyond it. Sometimes, especially in the early morning or in the evening, they saw great sea creatures sporting among the waves. They wished they could get past the Colossus and hunt the seas, as they had been trained to do. If they could get just one of those creatures they saw diving and rolling out there, they could carve off enough meat to last them a month and use the bones to make things. But the Colossus stood gravely, as if waiting for them to make a break for it so he could kill someone else.

After a few weeks, Bertram Wesley, who had been the ship's carpenter, disappeared. They all thought he was dead. They went searching for him in the forest, calling his name. They found him a half a mile away, hacking at a huge tree trunk with his ax. Over the next week, Bertram Wesley's project took form: It was a monument of the Colossus that had killed their shipmate.

"That's the statue you found overgrown!" Javi said.

Yoshi nodded.

A little shiver went through Javi. That statue had looked ancient. But these sailors saw it when it was new, just hewn out of the tree.

In his journal, Sammy wrote: *It was done beautiful. Bertram used to be apprenticed to a carver of ship's figureheads—making mermaids, and seamen, and Ohio as a young lady, and the like. This Colossus is carved as good as any ship's figurehead. It's a monument to all of us who died of starvation on the ship, and Mr. Cressy, who was killed by the Colossus, and Mr. Onslow, who saved us all and died at the falls. On the base of the statue, Bertram writ,* "In Memory of the Crew of the Whaler *LaRue." And in big letters:* "FATE TREADS UPON US ALL." *Someday it will be in memory of the four of us, too. It will stand after we're gone.*

One night when Muller was playing his concertina, several birds—they must have been slide-whistle birds—landed near them to listen to the song. Mr. Scarlett picked up his spear, and that night they had meat as part of their diet. That revolutionized their exile in this alien Eden.

A few days later they found what they called the *metal halo*—one of the alien control devices. From their perch in the trees, they spotted a circle of particularly tall growth and set out to see it. What they found was a gravity bubble, though they didn't understand it or call it that. *We leaped and soared like angels, until we attracted the deadly attentions of the knife birds.* They retreated outside the circle, but not before they'd noticed a metal ring set in the dirt. Sammy crawled in to investigate it while the shredder birds flocked, clattered, and screeched in the air right above him. He ran his fingers across the symbols on the ring and found himself triple his own weight. He couldn't hold himself up. He touched the ring again, and found he had *broken its magic spell*—he weighed no more or less than usual. He brought the *halo* back to the others.

Over the next few days, they explored its powers, though they suspected it was an artifact of witchcraft or wizardry.

"Look," Javi said. "Sammy drew the symbols on the alien device right here. Look at these . . . They're the same symbols that appeared on the ring we found just after the crash. He and the crew were trying to figure out what each one does."

Yoshi tugged the book out of Javi's hands and ran his finger across the symbols. "Yeah," he agreed. "You're right."

"They got the gravity setting immediately. Next, this symbol here is the one we've used to flood tech with energy or drop the energy level."

"Like when you guys blew up the plane?" said Yoshi.

Javi ignored him. "They didn't figure that one out at all. Sammy just wrote a question mark next to it. They also didn't get the one that Hank used to speed up time. Next to this one, Sammy writes, *This makes water into an ice that is not cold, but can be carried.* That's the one the Cub-Tones used to store water."

Like the Cub-Tones, the survivors of the *LaRue* began to fall into a routine. They trapped and ate birds using Muller's concertina and traps they set in the bushes. There were a few other animals they found to be edible, though some made them sick. They learned which berries were good. They ended up feeding some strange forest creature and making a pet out of it, a faithful mammal that appeared to be a cross between a bear cub and a nickel-plated telescope. Sammy named it Jonah. It went everywhere with him, running and hunting, curling up by his side.

They actually managed to harpoon a dreadful duck, and this is when the "metal halo" came in use again: They used it to refrigerate the meat in the water cubes. Something about the congealing effect of the device slowed the rot. They found they could live for a full week off the duck's body. "Except they served me the brain," Sammy complained, "because I am the smallest. It was not a big-brained bird."

One evening, they returned to camp late, having spent the whole day hunting an elephant-pig. It was dark when they got back. They lit a fire and prepared to cook the wild pig. Muller sat playing them tunes while they cooked. It was a good evening. They had plenty to eat. They sang about their loved ones, off across the wide salt sea: their girlfriends in many ports, their mothers and fathers back home on their farms, their sisters and brothers in the great cities of the world.

The fire cast a warm red light over their huts. When the flames grew higher, the men could see up to the treetops and into the dark woods.

And they could see a glint of metal. A huge shadow.

The Colossus was standing at the edge of the hollow, watching them.

Waiting for them.

The music of the concertina died with a sick shriek.

The monster stepped out of the shadows. The earth jolted with its weight.

Sammy discovered he was yelling in panic. He grabbed Jonah the telescope-cub and ran, while behind him, the Colossus shot bolts of blue fire at the huts. They exploded in sudden bursts of flame.

The creature strode forward. The men scattered, yelling, almost crazed in fear.

The only person who remained behind was Muller. He was done with running. Maybe he was done with everything. Sammy screamed his name and called for him to run, but Muller stood his ground, facing the Colossus with a look of hate in his eyes, prepared to die. With his mouth in a snarl of defiance, he began to play a hymn: "Farewell, My Friends, I'm Bound for Canaan." He clearly thought it would be a good thing to play during his last minutes on Earth.

Sammy begged, "No, Muller! No!"—but then shut himself up, because he didn't want the monster to hear him. With Jonah quivering in his arms, he turned and kept running.

He leaped through spiky alien brambles.

He had gone quite a ways when he realized that he could still hear the music. Muller was still playing the hymn. Somehow, Muller had not been killed.

Sammy paused. He wasn't proud of himself for running. It might have been the right thing to do, but it had not been a brave thing to do.

Then the hymn ended, and the concertina fell silent.

There was another sickening monster step—a crunch.

Muller! Oh, Muller! thought Sammy to himself.

But then the concertina quickly started up again, playing the same tune. "Farewell, My Friends, I'm Bound for Canaan . . ." This time faster, as if in panic.

Sammy wondered exactly what was going on. Did the monster like the music?

And then the Colossus sang back, in a voice like a church organ. Its tune was ugly, high, and strange, like no other music Sammy had ever heard.

But it did not kill Muller.

Instead, it turned and stomped back into the darkness it had come from. It headed back to the beach.

Sammy and the others crept out of their hiding places. Muller sat, carefree, on the pile of their ruined huts, playing an Irish song about whisky. He knew lots of those.

"Didn't hurt a hair on my head," he boasted, grinning. "Who'd've thought that the old Colossus would know a good old New England hymn?"

Bertram protested, "How in Heaven and Earth did you ever tame the demon?"

"I'm a lovely player on the concertina. I've soothed bar fights from Boston to San Francisco."

Sammy had a different idea. "Maybe something that you played was a signal," he suggested. "Like when bugles play on the battlefield."

"Aye," said Mr. Scarlett, who had fought as a boy in the American Civil War. "The trumpets sound the advance and the retreat and all manner of other commands. I think, friend Muller, you found a way to talk to the mighty Colossus."

The next morning, Sammy and Muller ran what Javi would have called an experiment.

They went to the beach. It was a foggy morning. The dark, towering shape of the Colossus could hardly be seen through the mist.

Muller went out with his concertina and stood about a hundred feet from the monster. The monster started walking toward him. Muller played an Irish dancing tune. The monster kept walking, raising its arms to smash him. He played a waltz. It kept on coming.

Quickly, Muller switched to the old hymn, "Farewell, My Friends, I'm Bound for Canaan."

The Colossus stopped. With its huge, whistling voice, it replied. Then it turned and went back to stand silently, looking out to the sea.

Muller crowed in triumph. They had figured out how to stop the creature from killing them.

That afternoon they built a raft, played the song for the Colossus, walked right past it, and went fishing.

"It's the key!" said Javi. "This is what we're looking for! Kimberly! Hey, Kimberly! Do you know any hymns?"

Kimberly came over. She shrugged. "Sure. I know some."

"I thought you would!" said Javi.

Yoshi explained, "Hymns stopped the cyborg from killing these sailors."

"A particular hymn," said Javi. "Do you know the song, 'Farewell, My Friends, I'm Bound for Canaan'?"

Kimberly squinted. "No. Sorry. I never heard of it."

Javi insisted, "You don't understand! If we knew that hymn, we could get past the Colossus any time we wanted!"

"Well, sorry, Javi," said Kimberly. "I'm in marching band. Not a choir."

"Maybe Hank will know," said Javi. "He's a composer."

"Maybe Hank will know what?" shouted Hank, hopping down the rocks from above with the others from the scouting party. They were back from keeping watch at the beach. Akiko and Anna both looked sunburned. But all five of them looked like they'd seen something incredible. Their eyes were wide, and they were breathing heavily from their jog back to the camp.

"What might I know?" Hank asked again.

"A hymn!" said Javi. "Called 'Farewell, My Friends, I'm Bound for Canaan'! Apparently those cyborgs love it!"

"Huh?" said Hank.

Anna announced, "We saw a robot battle! It's not just us that the cyborg wants to kill!"

Hank said, "She's not lying. Some mites came out of the sea and the cyborgs all had a big fight with them and destroyed them all."

"It was crazy, man!" Crash said. He clearly had enjoyed a great afternoon of mechanized battle.

"Whoa," said Javi. "Well, I guess we made it to the robot soccer finals after all. Just a little more violent than we expected."

Anna said, "I think I know what the cyborgs are doing. I figured it out while we were walking to the beach. I was looking at the different kinds of trees, and thinking about survival and evolution, and suddenly I realized why the cyborgs keep watch on the shore like that."

Molly asked, "Why's that, Anna?"

"They're guarding their biomes."

Molly frowned. "Okay? Meaning?"

"Each of the environments we've been in feels completely different, right? I mean, we were in the jungle first, and then desert, and then the Cub-Tones' forest, and now the blue broccoli forest. And then there's the sea. The endorheic basin. And they all feel kind of artificial, right? Like they're much closer together than you'd expect?"

People nodded.

"Yeah," Molly agreed. "Kind of like in a terrarium or a greenhouse or something."

Anna said, "Each one is a specific biome, a particular set of plants and animals that somehow work together to survive. Usually, a desert would cover hundreds or thousands of square miles. Here, it's just a little sample biome that covered, what, maybe twenty square miles."

"Sure," said Hank. "Where are you going with this?"

"Those cyborgs are guarding *this* biome, because it's still being grown. It's not complete yet."

"How can you tell it's not complete?" asked Kimberly, impressed.

"Because this forest is pretty new. I don't know how new— all the trees are alien—but you can tell it used to be like the Cub-Tones' forest. Look at the fallen trees or the ones down here that the old tree houses are built in. They're more like the last environment. They're not blue broccoli."

Javi asked, "So why are the cyborgs guarding it?"

"Because it's new," Anna insisted. "It's still not fully formed. It's still growing. It hasn't reached its equilibrium. The cyborgs don't want anything to mess it up while it's still fragile. Biomes are really carefully balanced, but they take a long time to achieve their balance. If you change one thing, everything changes. If one animal is introduced that wasn't there, the whole biome can change. For example, English settlers took rabbits to Australia for food. It turned out that rabbits were really well-suited to live in Australia."

"And rabbits make lots of rabbits," Javi pointed out.

"So pretty soon, the rabbits had taken over a lot of the environments that used to be filled with other animals. Rabbits changed the whole system."

Yoshi leaned against a tree. "You think the cyborgs are trying to stop rabbits?"

"I think the cyborgs are trying to stop anything from crossing over the boundaries between biomes."

Hank was confused. "But what about the little robot mites? They're protecting this place, too, right?"

Anna looked surprised. "Oh," she said. "That's a good point. So far the mites we've seen have been maintaining the biomes, and especially the technology here. They're part of the same system."

"But wait," said Javi. "Back at the edge of the desert, the mites were the ones that tried to keep us from breaking out of the jungle. They were policing the edge of the biome. But here, it's the little robots that were trying to cross the boundary and the cyborgs that were stopping them."

Molly put a hand on her forehead and stared down at the ground. "Okay. Let's think about this. This isn't the first time we've suspected there are competing . . . sides, I guess . . . to the rift. Dana saw it before any of us did. I think by now it's clear that we're not just up against one force—whoever's maintaining these biomes and trapping us in them. We're up against two. The makers and the unmakers, say. And they're fighting each other. That's important."

"Really important," said Javi. "Because one side might want to help us . . . and the other side might be trying to kill us."

Molly nodded firmly. "And it will be up to us to figure out if we can somehow use their war against each other to get out of this alive."

There was a long, thoughtful silence.

Then Kimberly said, "Wowzers."

16

Molly

It was terrifying to think of unknown forces battling it out around them. But on the other hand, Molly realized, at least now they were getting closer to a solution that made sense. She liked solutions.

"The sailors thought the cyborg was like the Colossus of Rhodes," Javi said, "a giant lighthouse in the form of a statue. But really, the Greek myth it's more like is Talos."

"Who's Talos?" Kimberly asked.

"The robotics team from Greece is named after him," Javi explained. "He was supposedly a giant robot built on the island of Crete in ancient times. He ran around the shores of the island, guarding it against pirates and invaders."

Molly wasn't thinking about ancient Greece, though. She was thinking about the future. She said, "If you're right, Anna, about some kind of force trying to create these alien biomes, then we need to stop and think for a second. Because this changes everything."

"Why?" asked Crash. "We still gotta get out of here."

Molly nodded. "We do, Crash, but we've got to worry about much more."

"What are you talking about?" asked Hank. "Spill the beans."

"Because what Anna is suggesting is that someone is trying to turn this part of the Earth into a replica of an alien world. Just like people talk about humans going to Mars and terraforming it—changing it so that it has air and Earth plants can grow on it. Someone from somewhere else has come to Earth and is planning on xenoforming it. Turning Earth into an *alien* world."

They all took this in for a minute.

"So far, only right here," said Hank. "Just in this rift."

"But maybe," Anna blurted, "soon covering the whole planet. This might be an invasion."

Javi shuddered. "Think about huge flocks of shredder birds flying through New York City. Hacking up people on Fifth Avenue."

"Or those giant guardians walking through Oregon," said Kimberly.

"Like Cal pictured," said Hank.

It was a terrifying image.

"But remember," said Hank, "that it seems like, if this really is people from Mars invading—"

"Or some other planet," said Javi.

"If it's *spacemen* invading, they're not all agreed on a plan. Somehow, they're fighting each other. Or themselves," said Hank. "That's our real hope."

Molly nodded. "Good point. We have to keep that in mind."

"So, gang," said Kimberly, "what does this mean about what we do next?"

Molly had no idea.

From over by the junk heap, Yoshi announced, "We shut down the Colossuses so they won't bother us again."

Javi rolled his eyes. "How?" he asked. "No one knows that song that stops them."

Yoshi smirked. "I do," he said. "I've been reading while you all have been chitchatting, and I've figured out the solution."

"What do you mean, Yoshi?" said Javi, sounding tired and exasperated. Molly could tell that he was a little jealous that Yoshi had read something he hadn't.

Yoshi explained to the group, "Okay, so there are these shipwrecked sailors. And they discover this one song stops the cyborg. Or the Colossus, as they call it. No other song works. So they keep on going back with this instrument, the concertina, whatever that is, and playing that one song. They made a raft from branches and some nets from dead tanglevine. And every day they went to the beach, played this song, got the Colossus to shut down, and then they went out to sea to fish. So every day, the guy who played the music figured out a little bit more what the Colossus liked in this song, and changed it a little bit."

"What did you say he was playing?" asked Hank.

"It's called a concertina," said Javi.

"It's like an accordion," Kimberly said. "A squeeze-box."

Hank thought about it for a second, and then something clicked. "Wait!" he said. "Wait! That machine we found! The 'Wannamaker'!" He scrambled up from the ground and ran over to the pile of broken things they'd searched through the previous day.

He pulled out a couple of metal hexagons. "These are the ends! These are parts of that guy's accordion!"

Kimberly came over and inspected them. "I bet you're right," she said.

Hank showed the group the hexagons, clearly proud he was an expert in something that turned out to be important. "In between these, there would have been a folded leather bellows."

"Why, sure!" Kimberly exclaimed. "The leather must have rotted years and years ago!"

Hank nodded. "If it *was* working, you'd squeeze the bellows open and closed. That forces air through these little tubes and makes sounds. These buttons here play the notes. That's clearly what this is!"

"And here," said Yoshi, swiveling the open book around so everyone could see it, "are the notes this guy figured out controlled the robot."

There on the page, in scratchy handwriting, the dead sailor Muller had written out the song he'd played to the Colossus.

"That's amazing, Yoshi!" Molly said. "But how will we fix the . . . what's it called?"

"Concertina," Kimberly offered.

"We don't need to," said Hank. "We'll play the song on my oboe or Akiko's flute. Is that okay?"

Yoshi explained what was going on to Kira and Akiko. Clearly, from the speed he was speaking, he was actually excited, though Molly could tell that when he spoke English, he was playing it cool.

Kira and Akiko looked delighted.

"Let's hear it!" said Javi. "I can't wait to hear cyborg dance tunes!"

Hank and Akiko got their instruments. They laid the diary out flat in front of them, and they both played the tune.

It wasn't long. Muller had written the music down in two forms: the original song and the slightly changed arrangement to suit the cyborg. In its form as a hymn, it was sad and mournful. He had written the words under the notes: *"Farewell, my friends . . . I'm traveling through the wilderness . . . I go away, behind to leave you, perhaps never to meet again. If we should never have the pleasure, we'll meet again in Heaven's land."*

Hank and Akiko played it beautifully, with a yearning sorrow, but frankly everyone was too excited to feel sad.

Then they played the second version, the perfected cyborg version. It was simpler, with some of the notes taken out. It didn't sound great, but it didn't have to sound good to human ears. Only the ears of the Colossus.

"We've got it!" said Molly. "Good work!"

Hank grinned. "So tomorrow," he said, "we give it a test, right?"

"We can't cross the water anyway," said Crash. "We don't have boats."

"Oh, yes, we do," said Molly. "Kimberly figured out we could use the pods of the fruit grenades as two-person canoes or kayaks. We could find smaller ones, bind them to sticks, and use them kind of like paddles."

"We can stop on the islands at night," Yoshi pointed out.

"As long as they don't turn out to be alive and hungry or crawling with killer robots, like everything else in this stupid place," said Crash.

Molly estimated, "It should only take us a couple of days to cross. We figured it was about six miles. That wouldn't take us much time at all if we had real boats and real paddles. Less than a day. But even with homemade paddles, we should be able to do it in a couple of days, tops."

"We can test the pod boats in the water tomorrow," Hank said. "After we neutralize the cyborgs."

"This is great!" said Javi.

Molly was happy and proud. They all felt like a team.

In the morning, they'd take the next big step of their voyage.

Yoshi

The campfire was almost fun that night. Hank and Kimberly played some music. Even though it was stupid music, Yoshi liked the sound of it.

He found himself sitting next to Anna. Yoshi couldn't help admiring her face and watching the way it reflected the firelight. She looked much more relaxed than usual.

Anna was a weird kid, there was no question about that. But something about the way she blurted stuff out made sense to Yoshi. She was true to herself. She didn't change her message depending on who she was talking to. If she thought you were going to die in the wilderness, she'd tell you.

Anna noticed him watching her. For a second, she looked confused. Then she picked up a stick and started to scratch the dirt. She said, "I wish I'd stayed up in the tree houses too. It must have been great to wake up there."

"Yeah," said Yoshi. "The sunrise was really nice."

"You must have been able to see all the way to other side of the sea."

"You can only see that there's land there. You can't see anything in particular."

"That sounds really cool, to wake up in the treetops at dawn."

"It was. I did my exercises up there."

"What kind of exercises? Jumping jacks? Those platforms look like they're held up by one nail."

"There are no nails. It's all pegs. And no, I do breathing exercises for my *kenjutsu*."

Anna's brow furrowed. "What's *kenjutsu*?"

"Japanese sword technique. It goes back to the time of the samurai. It's not just about slashing stuff up."

"You do a lot of slashing stuff up."

"Only because you guys are always so stupid."

Anna rolled her eyes. "So you practice breathing?"

"Yeah. You center yourself. It makes a big difference if you strike when you're breathing in or when you're breathing out."

"I've heard you shout things when you swing your sword."

"My katana, yeah."

"Your katana. You shout words."

Yoshi liked the fact that she'd watched him so closely. He said, "It's a concentration thing."

"What are you concentrating on?"

"It's called *kiai,* the force you bring against your opponent. It's in your breath. It's in your body. It's in the shout. It's your whole force. It's in your spirit, your *ki*. When you're really good, even if you don't speak or move, the force of your *kiai* can convince an opponent that you're advancing."

"That's amazing. How do you breathe right?"

Yoshi put his hand on his stomach. "From here, not from up in your chest." He breathed slowly, in and out, watching his own hand rise and fall.

"Yoshi!" barked Kira, from across the fire. "Akiko just had a good idea. We need to you to translate for Molly."

"I'll be there in a minute," said Yoshi.

Anna was puffing in and out, holding her belly. "Like this?" she asked.

"No. Your stomach should rise when you breathe in, and sink when you breathe out." Yoshi reached over and put his hand on her hand to show her.

Anna blinked, startled.

Yoshi pulled his hand away. "I'm sorry. I didn't mean . . ."

"No, that's okay."

"Really. Sorry." He shook his head.

Anna stared straight in his eyes. As if she barely dared, she said, "Show me."

Yoshi nodded. He reached over, and—

"Yoshi!" Kira said, standing right next to him. "What are you doing? We need to talk to Molly."

Yoshi sat up straight. He could feel himself blushing, like he'd been caught doing something wrong. All he was doing was showing Anna how to breathe . . .

"I had an idea," said Akiko. "Sorry to bother you. But I was thinking about boats, and I realized that it would be easier to ride in those seed pods if we tied a few of them together with sticks, like catamarans or pontoon boats."

Yoshi didn't know what any of these things were, and he didn't really care.

"Okay," he said.

"They'll be more stable if we tied them together," Kira said. "Think of three pods side by side. Two people ride in the middle one. The pods on each side will stop the boat from tipping over." She showed a sketch she'd just done. "It was Akiko's idea."

"Great," said Yoshi.

"We need to show Molly," said Akiko.

"So show her."

"We have to explain it!" said Akiko.

Kira insisted. "We need a translator."

"I'm not a translator."

"No. You're a jerk." Kira turned and walked off.

Akiko followed her, looking disappointed.

"I've got to go," Yoshi said to Anna.

"Okay," said Anna, crestfallen.

Yoshi hesitated. He sucked in a gulp of air and admitted, "I wish you could have seen the sunrise from the treetops, too." Then he walked away, feeling like an idiot for saying that. Why did one of these nerds confuse him like this?

He must be losing his edge.

18

Javi

That night, Javi couldn't sleep. He was too excited about trying out the song and getting past the Colossus the next day.

Instead of sleeping, he scanned the rest of the journal of the *LaRue*. There wasn't enough time to read every story in it, every adventure. The writing was too small and went in too many directions. But he wanted to find out what happened to Sammy Cardosa, cabin boy.

In the weeks that followed the discovery of the Colossus's song, the remaining crew settled into a new pattern. Bertram Wesley, an expert woodworker, made them a small boat. They would go out in the morning, play their hymn for the Colossus, and then head out to fish. Once, they went back to the spot where the *LaRue* had plunged to its doom. They wandered over the rocks at the base of the waterfall, picking out pieces of wood, metal appliances, and other things that might be useful.

They experimented with the antigravity setting on the halo device they'd found in the forest. It was almost impossible to use for long periods because of the shredder birds, but it did allow them to lift timbers high up into the trees. They built houses in the treetops, so they wouldn't be menaced at night by dreadful ducks (which they called *dragon birds*). They were used to climbing rigging, so they made rope ladders of tightly wound vine. They whittled the bones of sea monsters to make little ornaments for their walls.

Years passed. They got older.

Bertram, the ship's carpenter, got bitten by a dragon bird. Horrified, they watched him turn into "a devil" over the next two weeks. He became confused and raved about cities full of monsters.

(Javi bit his lip. This was the very same thing that was happening to Cal. He read on.)

Late one night, Sammy was asleep in the tree house. Everything was still.

And then something leaped on him, strangling him, trying to push him off the deck. Some new horror, up in the trees.

No: It was Bertram. Insane. Murderous.

Sammy kicked the man in the stomach, fighting for air, and reached for his herring knife.

Mr. Scarlett leaped over a bridge and grabbed Bertram's arms. Bertram was strangely strong. He screamed, "You're ruining it all! You're ruining it! Maintenance is in damage mode!"

(As Javi read this, he sucked in his breath.)

Bertram craned his neck to bite Mr. Scarlett—and together, the two of them fell from the tree.

Sammy and Muller swarmed down the rope ladder. Mr. Scarlett was broken but still alive—and Bertram was still trying to kill him, shrieking in a high, musical voice that he would cleanse the place of all of them.

Javi stopped reading. Was this what Cal would eventually do? He had already attacked his friends in the Cub-Tones once, destroying their instruments. And he was getting worse, even in the short time they'd left the Cub-Tones' compound. He was becoming stranger. Could they trust him at night anymore?

Javi looked over at the green boy. Cal wasn't sleeping. He was squatting on the ground, blinking with red eyes into the night. Not very reassuring.

Molly was also awake. She caught Javi's eye.

Javi looked back down at the page.

Muller and Sammy managed to pull Bertram away from Mr. Scarlett. He lashed out at them, but they held him. They bound his hands and his feet together. One of his legs had been broken in the fall, and he screamed with pain. Mr. Scarlett was whimpering. They thought his back might be broken.

They didn't know what to do with Bertram. He was dangerous, even tied up and wounded. They decided to take him up to one of the tree houses and cut it off from the rest. They would imprison him there until they could make a final decision.

He had to be lifted with the gravity device. Sammy and Muller leaped up with him, pulling themselves up the tree, light as air. All the while, he swung his head around, trying to bite them.

Once they got him up to the hut, they started to pull up the bridge that connected it to the other tree houses.

Sammy turned and found that Bertram had broken out of his bonds. He'd grabbed the antigravity device. He was grinning wildly and touching its symbols.

He kicked off from the platform and spun above the tree-tops. "I'm flying again!" he crowed. "You can't keep me anywhere! I'll—"

And then the shredder birds found him. He screamed.

Sammy wanted to help him somehow, but there was nothing to do. Even if they could save him, he would try to kill them. The shredder birds clustered around him, shooting back and forth, growling. Bertram screamed, fluting weird notes, until he fell silent.

Torn to shreds, Bertram's body slowly drifted down to the ground as if it were no heavier than paper.

"I can't read much more of this," Javi whispered to Molly.

"What's wrong?" Molly asked.

"They just had to kill a guy who was turning into a monster, like Cal."

Molly's eyes grew wide. "What?"

"Yeah. He went nuts and tried to murder them all."

"But why did they have to *kill* him? Why couldn't they just, I don't know, imprison him or something, like Hank did? Cal isn't dangerous. He's just confused."

"I know," said Javi. "I know! But these guys, they were serious about surviving, and he attacked them." Javi looked across the fire at Cal. "I wonder if Cal's going to snap like that. And what'll we do then?"

Molly drew up her legs and shivered.

She stared into the fire. She said, "You wouldn't kill Cal, would you? It's not his fault he's turning into a monster."

Javi shrugged. "I don't know. It would depend on what he did. But you're the boss."

"Uh-huh," said Molly. "I'm the boss."

Javi turned back to the book.

There were other stories in the book, clearly, but Javi didn't have time to read all of them. He'd go back if necessary. He wanted to find out what finally happened to the crew.

He flipped through the pages, looking for the latest date on an entry. Sammy stopped keeping the diary regularly. Sometimes, Javi could only find a single entry for a whole year. He skipped ahead . . . *1900 . . . 1910 . . . 1915* . . . Somewhere, the First World War was going on—machine guns rattling in trenches and bombs blowing up churches—and Sammy knew none of it, trapped in the otherworldly jungle.

1920 . . . 1931 . . . Javi kept looking for the last dates.

Sammy no longer mentioned anyone else except Jonah, his strange pet. *Jonah and I planted more berry bushes today. I planted and Jonah watched . . . Cut my hand today. Worried about it turning bad. Jonah licked the wound. Don't know if that's good.*

1942 . . . Now the Second World War was going on, and Sammy was still locked here, safe, in this valley. He must have been an old man. Javi only had to look up to see Sammy's marks on the trees, the counting of days, weeks, months, years, hanging all around them in the dark.

Then Javi found the final entry. It was surrounded by black crosses. Sammy's handwriting was so shaky it was hard to read. Javi held it near the fire and squinted. It said:

I, Sammy Cardosa, in the 73rd year of my age, believe I have come to the final shore, and shall soon hear the Captain call me to set sail for the last time, and make the final voyage into the darkness.

I remember that there was once a world with buildings and horses and ladies who danced. I was fourteen when I left that world, and now I am an old man with a long white beard. I have lived my life in this place. I grew into manhood here, and now I will die here. I can barely remember cities. The others talked to me about them. For twenty-three years, I have spoken to no other human soul. I talk only to Jonah, who does not seem to age. For some time, I have thought he is not all animal, but also a machine, perhaps a way for someone to watch over me. Strange, then, that he has remained such a good companion, and he shall be the one thing I miss when I pass on from this world to another.

I am sick, and have no desire to see the sun rise again or the moons set. I will lie in the boat Bertram Wesley built us and I will let myself die. I have no strength to get water anymore or to boil it.

For years, we waited to be rescued. Then one day I realized that I was forty-five years old, and that this was my home. Who wants to be rescued from their home? I know the ways of this place. How would I fetch a meal in a city where I do not need to play a tune for the Colossus? Would I find New York so charming after I have slept through a storm in that crystal chamber under the Earth, where the walls all sing?

Javi had no idea what this was, but figured it was some other story he hadn't read, or that Sammy hadn't written down.

No. I do not need to be rescued anymore. Sometimes we belong where we find ourselves. I will sleep here with Jonah at my side, and before another day passes, my rescue will come: my crew members will haul me up by a rope and greet me as if the years have not passed. We will begin this last voyage together.

The Captain sets a course for the rising sun.

Samuel Cardosa

aet. 73 years

Here sets down his pen

Javi closed the book. Hank was improvising on the oboe and Crash was beating out rhythms with kindling.

Javi didn't want to hear music.

He wanted to get out of this place.

He wanted it worse than he'd ever wanted anything in this life.

They had only one chance.

19

Yoshi

The next day, they walked along the wide path, bold and triumphant.

It was about time. Yoshi felt like he didn't have time for other people's fear anymore. He had learned he could take care of himself. He wasn't a kid anymore. He was a swordsman. He wasn't just a *hafu* anymore—half Japanese, half white. He was himself, he was Yoshi, and that was something to be proud of.

They walked in a big gang, carrying the giant emptied seed pods between them.

Javi and Molly were laughing together. Javi said, "Feels like going to the beach when we were kids. Walking from the parking lot over the dunes with our floaties."

Molly remembered, "You had an inner tube or something shaped like a dinosaur."

"I loved that thing!" said Javi. "I couldn't believe that you wanted a pool float without teeth. Yours was just blue. No eyes or anything."

Yoshi wished they'd be quiet instead of yapping about floaties like a couple of little kids.

Hank and Akiko led the way. They had their instruments at the ready. They had memorized the two tunes—both the original and the version Muller said the Colossus liked better. Unlike Molly and Javi, Hank and Akiko looked very serious. Yoshi appreciated that. Molly was in charge; she should be focused, not joking around.

Now Molly and Javi were talking about how hot the blacktop of the beach parking lot used to be, and how they would worry that the soles of their feet were going to burn off. They'd run into the ocean together, screaming to cool their heels.

Even to Yoshi, Javi's family sounded kind of fun. He got a sense that there were a lot of them, and that they were loud and did a lot of stuff together.

But on the other hand, thought Yoshi, it had made Javi kind of goofy. The kid was smart, but he couldn't protect himself. His feelings were always out in the open.

And now they were *all* out in the open: They'd reached the beach.

As soon as they gathered on the shore, the nearest cyborg started to stalk toward them.

"Okay. Get ready," said Molly. Now she was all business, lips tight and eyes fixed on the enemy. "Hank and Akiko, get into position. Prepare to play."

"Sure," said Hank, frowning. "We know."

"Everyone," Molly continued, "get ready to scatter and run if it doesn't work. No one's getting flattened today."

The cyborgs had all taken notice. One was stomping toward them from each side.

It wasn't going to be easy to escape if the plan failed, Yoshi realized.

Akiko and Hank started Muller's song. It cried out on the morning wind, punctuated by the growling cries of lone shredder birds.

It was kind of beautiful, but Yoshi was ready for action.

They reached the end of the song. The cyborgs didn't stop.

Quickly, Hank and Akiko started the old, original version.

That didn't work, either.

They played Muller's version again.

"Get ready to run!" said Molly, her voice tight with anxiety. "This isn't working!"

The cyborgs raised their arms and prepared to fire.

"RUN!" said Molly, and everyone burst in a pack toward the forest.

No sooner had they moved than blue bolts of fire struck the sand, kicking up clouds.

Yoshi made sure the others were in front of him. He felt ready to take on anyone and anything. He drew his katana.

The others had made it off the beach and into the forest. Not Yoshi.

Defiantly, he faced the two giants.

They aimed right at him.

Time to move evasively. Using his *kenjutsu* training, Yoshi leaped from side to side, moving backward in a tactical retreat.

A blast hit the beach nearby, sweeping him with a rooster tail of sand and pebbles. He staggered, but still managed to leap with the explosion, hurling himself toward the forest.

The two cyborgs now stood shoulder to shoulder. They paced toward him.

It was time to run. He'd find a way to deactivate these things later—but this was not the moment.

Yoshi charged into the forest, at once feeling how exposed his back was and how he loved running in the midst of danger.

He just wished it didn't feel like he was crawling, given that each step of the giants covered fifteen of his own.

He heard the others call his name.

"Keep going!" Yoshi shouted. "They're chasing me!"

He wished the others wouldn't get in his way. He could take care of himself.

He bounded into the trees and started jumping over fallen trunks.

A quick glance behind told him the cyborgs had stopped at the verge of the woods. They were poised there, watching to see what he did.

From what Anna said, the most important thing was to get away from the beach—and the edge of the biome.

Once he was back in the jungle, the cyborgs let him run.

He ran in what he knew was a wide arc, so they wouldn't be able to trace him back to the grove with its tree houses. By the time he got back to the others, he was covered in sweat, but it was a good sweat, a sweat that meant he'd worked hard and well.

He stood, breathing sharply. Kimberly offered him a water blob to drink from. He sipped deeply, calming himself, centering himself.

Suddenly, he felt someone's eyes on him.

Anna. She was staring at him.

The moment he looked back at her, she looked away.

Yoshi felt something. He didn't know what. He closed his eyes and concentrated on breathing.

For all his courage, looking at Anna just then seemed like more than he could handle.

Molly said, "Thoughts? Conclusions?"

"Yeah," said Javi. "We were completely wrong. We're stuck here. We're screwed."

20

Molly

To make things worse, it rained hard that afternoon. Everyone was soaked. They scrunched under the open pods they had planned to use as boats. Molly, Javi, and Cal huddled beneath the rib-bone table.

Yoshi sat out in the open, soaked, with the rain falling right on him. He gazed angrily in the direction of the beach, thinking private thoughts.

Kimberly's voice came from under her pod. "Yoshi! Come on and get under something!"

He just replied, "It's a warm rain," and wouldn't say anything more.

Javi was talking quietly with Molly about extracting the explosive from the grenade fruit.

Molly said, "We'd need to keep some of the flesh of the fruit on hand to mix with it. That's when it actually explodes. Of course, it's also good to eat."

"I can't believe you ate so much of it," said Javi.

"It is a feast for the stomach," Cal twittered. "Good as a salad or sauce."

"You've been eating it, too?" Javi said.

"It is a feast for the stomach," Cal repeated. He scratched his rough green hide and curled up to sleep.

Molly knew that her skin looked more like that every day. The infection was spreading. If they didn't find a solution within a few days, she would turn into something else entirely. At this rate, she had less than a week left of being human.

She couldn't concentrate on Javi's discussion of draining the fruit pimples of their explosive juice. She was too worried for herself.

She thought of her mother, alone. A hundred times since the crash, she'd pictured what her mom must have gone through when the call came: *Mrs. Davis, we have some bad news. The plane that your daughter was on has disappeared somewhere over the Arctic . . .*

Molly was the last person her mother had. Her mom must have crumpled on the floor when she learned her daughter had gone down in the plane crash. Must have wailed. Like Molly felt like doing now.

Molly wished she could just tell her mom, *Whatever happens, I did my best. I was surrounded by friends.* She wished she could tell her mom to stay strong.

Javi had stopped talking and was watching one of the empty seed pods bumping and scuttling toward them.

"Who's that?" said Javi.

It tipped up. Underneath it was Anna.

"Molly," she whispered. Molly could hardly hear her over the pounding rain.

"You don't have to whisper, Anna."

"Yes, I do." She pulled herself closer to Molly under the table. "Yesterday, when I went out with Hank to watch the cyborgs, after the robot battle, Akiko and Kira and I came up behind the boys before they knew we were there. Hank was trying to get Crash to agree to join him if . . . if he ever overthrew you."

Molly felt her belly flop. *"Overthrew* me?"

"That wasn't the word Hank used. But if there was ever a chance to change leaders."

"You think that's what Hank's planning?"

"That's what he said."

Molly looked around the campsite at the kids huddled under shells.

"What's Hank doing right now?"

"He's reading the journal," Anna answered. "He wants to see if there's anything about the music that Javi and Yoshi might have missed."

"That makes sense," said Molly. She tried to remind herself that they were all in this mess together. "He's just feeling bad because his own team doesn't trust him anymore. And after being a leader for all those months—"

"Years," Anna corrected.

"—it must be tough to meet us, kids who come from the future and know more about science and how the world works."

But then, after having defended Hank, Molly thought a bit more. How desperate was Hank to lead, exactly? She turned to Anna. "You'll stick with me if he tries to take over the group, right?"

"Of course! Killbots forever!"

Javi, overhearing them, repeated, "Killbots forever!"

Molly lowered her head onto her crossed arms and knees. "But maybe it would be better if someone else took control. Apparently, I'm not such a great leader."

"Yes, you are!" Javi said. "You always think about other people."

"But look at where we are," Molly said. And she added mentally: *And we don't even know how long I'll be sane.* She could almost feel the thick, soupy infection coursing through her veins, like some kind of alien blood. She felt the new spurs of bone and cartilage that were growing in her hips and shoulders. She looked at Cal, curled up and green.

Even if they escaped this tropical prison in the Arctic wastes—even if they got back to New York—by the time she walked through the familiar door of her apartment, what would she be? Would she be herself at all?

Later that afternoon, when the rain finally slowed, Javi, Kimberly, and Anna went off to try to drain some explosive juice out of the fruit pimples. They wanted to experiment. Hank was still hunched under a pod shell, reading the journal. Akiko and Kira joined Molly under the table, shivering, and they shared the warmth of the battery.

As water dripped down the blue broccoli stalks, Molly fell asleep. Akiko and Kira whispered to each other in languages Molly didn't understand. Soon, in Molly's dream, a third voice, a new voice, added to theirs, this one singing to her. She couldn't tell what it was saying, either, but it seemed to be trying to tell her something through song.

She dreamed about high towers and cities built on impossible cliffs. She dreamed of intense cold. Ice and falling and broken limbs.

The pain jolted her awake.

As soon as she woke up, the pain was gone. Just a dream. Akiko was holding her hand, saying with concern, "Okay? Molly?"

She must have screamed out.

"You heard it," Cal said, watching her with wide eyes from several feet away.

"What are you talking about, Cal?" Molly asked warily.

Cal pointed to the battery. "It calls to us."

At first, Molly didn't know what he was talking about.

And then it hit her.

The dreams.

When did they happen?

She thought back: The dream of flying. This dream, most recently.

They happened when she slept near the battery.

What if.

It was. Not.

A battery.

She grabbed it and held it up, shaking it. "Cal, what is this? What is it really?"

Akiko and Kira were looking at her with wide eyes. Though they couldn't understand the specifics, they could tell she had just figured something out, and that she was frightened.

Cal said, "It calls to us."

"What calls to us?"

"From the end of the valley."

"Cal, this isn't really a battery, is it?"

"Walkie-talkie," he agreed.

Molly nodded. "Like a walkie-talkie."

It all made sense: Anna, Kira, and Yoshi had gotten the "battery" from the smashed casing of a robot. They had all just assumed that, because it created warmth, it was the robot's battery. But no—it was something more important than that. It was a communications device.

"You said something was calling us, Cal. From the end of the valley. What's calling to us when we're asleep?"

Cal stared at her with steady, unblinking eyes.

He answered, "The thing that we're becoming."

21

Anna

Now that the rain was over, the forest dripped quietly.

Anna, Kimberly, and Javi were working on trying to isolate the explosion juice. As they gathered hollow reeds to act as tubing, Javi sang a jingle for a made-up ad, "Yeah, yeah, yeah! It's a fruit explosion!"

Kimberly thought he was hilarious.

They sliced the reeds into points to pierce the bomb pimples. He sang, "Hold on to your sox! It's like a juice box! And a straw, but it's deadly!"

"What's a juice box?" Kimberly asked.

"Not worth it to explain," said Javi. "I'll buy you one when we get back to civilization. Along with something called Cheetos. For you, it'll be a futuristic feast. I'm a great date."

Kimberly held up an old frying pan as a shield while Javi carefully tried to poke a hole in one of the fruit zits.

"This is a bad idea," he muttered to himself as the first reed crumpled. "My cousin who lost the two fingers had to learn how to type again." He darted another sharpened reed at the bump. This time it sliced through.

There was a loud *crack!* and Kimberly and Javi fell backward. Javi was groaning in pain. Both he and Kimberly were bleeding.

Anna ran over. Javi's hand had been sliced up by seedlings and he'd been struck by the frying pan as it flew backward. Javi writhed in pain. Kimberly was crying, holding up her hand, which was red and burned.

Anna threw her a canteen. "Put water on it!" she shouted. "Quick!"

Anna grabbed some of the healing salve that Dana from the Cub-Tones had made for their journey. She handed it to Kimberly, who began to slather it on, stopping every few seconds to open and close her fist in pain.

Others came running. "What's going on?" Hank called.

"We were trying to get out some of the explosive in the fruits," Anna explained. "I think we made a mistake. It wasn't reacting with the flesh of the fruit. It was reacting with the air."

"You idiots," Yoshi growled.

Anna inspected Kimberly's hand. "It's burned," Kimberly said through gritted teeth. "It's really badly burned." She winced, but was still trying to be helpful. "Isn't that important to know about the chemical, that it burns?"

"It's not just burned," Anna blurted out. "You have contusions. Your blood vessels burst under the skin. The pressure of the explosion must have broken them all. It'll probably hurt a lot more."

Javi was still bent over, rocking with the pain of being burned, stabbed with wood splinters, and slapped with a frying pan. He was covered in red goo from the fruit.

"Whose idea was this?" Hank demanded. "It could have been even worse."

Javi coughed and said, "I thought we could make the stuff into a bigger bomb. Or even use it for a combustion engine. To get our boats across the sea. Well, one thing: Molly's not wrong about the fruit. Some of the goo went in my mouth. It's tangily delicious."

"We can't even get our boats into the sea," Kimberly said, downhearted.

"Oh, yes, we can," said Hank. He grinned.

Molly asked, "What do you mean?"

Hank held up the book he had been reading. His finger was still stuck in between two pages, holding his place. "Because while you've been playing mad scientists, I've been reading the journal from the *LaRue*. And I think I've figured out what we did wrong when we were playing Muller's song."

Despite the pain, Javi unbent himself, eager to hear. "What is it? What did we do?"

"Get yourself cleaned up and smeared with Dana's healing jelly. Then let's all talk."

In a few minutes, when Javi and Kimberly had bound up their wounds in healing salve, the whole group met around the table of ribs. Everyone was anxious to hear what Hank had to say. He was riding high, grinning at everyone, proud of his deduction.

"The key is here," he said, opening to a page of Sammy's journal. "Just after the shipwreck. Before they encounter the Colossus. Okay, listen to this:

It is night. We are sitting at the bottom of the cliff. We have salvaged some of the wreckage of the gallant LaRue. *Muller is playing us a tune on the concertina to remember the brave crew, our fine captain, and Mr. Onslow, who saved our lives.*

Muller's concertina was damaged when he was escaping from the ship. One of the reeds is cracked and makes a constant whine as he plays. Still, it is comforting to have the music we remember here in this strange and forbidden land where we are trapped.

The cabin boy of the LaRue, *youngest and most foolish of those on the ship, salvaged this journal, so that a full record might be kept of our voyages. He has taken up the pen from where the great Mr. Onslow left off just yesterday. Forgive a cabin boy for taking on this duty, but all the others say they do not want to write of what has happened.*

So we all prepare ourselves to explore this place where we are stranded. We are determined to make it back to our home shores, and then this record will tell our story.

Though it is written by the least of all, a mere child, your servant,

Sammy Cardosa, cabin boy.

"Yeah, sure," said Yoshi. "We read that before."

Hank smiled. "But you didn't read it like a musician."

"So are you going to sing it?" Javi asked sarcastically. "Want Crash to lay down a rhythm track?"

Crash scrunched up his nose in confusion. "What's a—" but Hank interrupted, eager to make his explanation.

"Muller's concertina was damaged. It was producing a high-pitched, extra note all the time. A drone, it's called."

Javi crinkled up his face. "Like the flying things that take pictures?"

"The what?" said Kimberly. "What planet are you from?"

"Never mind," said Javi. "I'm guessing this is a different kind of drone."

Hank explained. "A drone is a long note that you just hold—like on a bagpipe—while you play a tune over it. And

I'm guessing that because the concertina was damaged, there was a drone sound—that high-pitched whine—when Muller played the Colossus his song." He looked around, but the group clearly didn't get it. "So *we weren't playing all the notes*. We weren't playing that drone. It must be important for the cyborg, as you call it, to recognize the song as part of its language. It needs to hear the drone, too."

Molly was getting excited. "Okay, Hank. Can we figure out which note this is that we were missing? Then you, Akiko, and Kimberly can play all the notes we need?"

"Maybe," Hank said. "Because we can look at the insides of the concertina. Maybe we can tell which note got squashed in the fall. That's the one that was probably sounding the drone."

They rushed to get the remains of the concertina.

An hour later, there was a band concert in the middle of the blue broccoli forest.

They played only one song. Slide-whistle birds settled around them to listen.

After they played it a few times, Hank stopped them, excited. "Swell!" he said. "Really swell!"

"What are you talking about?" said Javi. "That sounded awful. That extra note you're playing is terrible. It makes me want to swat Kimberly like a mosquito."

"It's not important whether it sounds good or not," Hank said. "I think I've figured out what must have been going on!"

"You already told us what was going on," growled Yoshi.

Hank said to Anna, Javi, and Molly, "You aren't the only ones with physics knowledge."

"Lay it on us," said Javi.

"When you play two high-pitched notes like this loud enough, sometimes it creates what's called a 'difference tone.' A note that's sort of partway between the two notes. It's an illusion; no one is actually playing the note you're hearing. But you can still hear it. And maybe the cyborgs could hear it. So the 'song' that's the code isn't the one that Muller was playing. It just so happened that part of that song—he never knew which part—created the right difference tones to make another, hidden song. Like a song written in invisible ink, in lemon juice, suddenly becoming audible." Hank turned to Akiko and Kimberly. "Play the drone note and the song again—but as loud and piercing as you can. Until it's almost painful. And everyone else listen for the difference tones."

Kimberly and Akiko blasted the tune. The woodwinds sounded shrill and terrible, buzzing in Anna's ears. She couldn't stand it. She covered her ears up. Yoshi grimaced like he'd just eaten rotten cheese. But Anna watched Javi's face light up. He had heard it.

"That's amazing!" said Javi. "It's like a ghost tune! It's kind of fluttery, and really inside your ears, instead of sounding like it comes from the instruments. It's like a ghost is whispering it to you."

"There you go," said Hank, smiling broadly. "Muller's ghost song. That's what's going to get us past the guard cyborgs on the beach."

Javi laughed. "Mateys," he said in a pirate accent, "we're a-goin' to sea."

22

Akiko

The next day at noon, as they went up to the sea, they did not talk. Kira whispered to her sister, "You're brave to play the ghost song. You're going to save us all."

"I'm not brave," Akiko explained. "This is going to work. I'm sure of it."

They slid their boats along the path beside them, dragging them with bungee cords and ropes of dead tanglevine. They were better prepared than last time. Using strong tree limbs, they had lashed three seed pods at a time together to make little catamarans, each one big enough for two people. It had been Kira and Akiko's suggestion, and they were proud of it. The engineers had been very excited about the idea, because they said it would make the boats more stable on the open water. It would be harder for the waves to tip them over.

On the other hand, they hadn't really figured out a way to make sails. None of them knew how to sail anyway. As a result, they would basically be paddling across the basin. It was not going to be quick work.

"I've never paddled before," Akiko told her sister. "My arms aren't very strong."

Kira smiled at her. "Strong enough," she said. "It's only six miles. Less than ten kilometers. We can make it. It's just a big lake."

A big lake with monsters in it, Akiko thought to herself. No one wanted to think too hard about what might be living under the dark green waves.

Kira said, "Yoshi says we'll spend tonight on an island."

Yoshi wasn't sharing a catamaran with anyone. He had made his own.

Akiko shook her head. "I wish Yoshi would calm down. He really is a nice person, when he tries."

Kira smiled. "I like him mean," she said.

"You would."

Yoshi called up to them. "Akiko, Molly is saying you and Kimberly should go up front with your flutes. Get ready to play Muller's ghost song."

"Sorry, sister," Akiko said to Kira. She let go of the vine rope and took out her flute. "You'll have to pull for yourself."

"This is going to be an important concert," Kira said. "Play well. Good luck."

They arrived at the beach.

Akiko felt impossibly tiny, now that she was faced with the slow waves crawling across the beach and the row of towering, headless sentinels. Kimberly smiled reassuringly at her.

Akiko nodded, and together they began blasting out the song. Kimberly played only one long, high, piercing note: the drone, like the broken note on the dead sailor's concertina. Akiko played the old melody as loud as she could.

The cyborgs started toward them, raising their arms for combat. They would not let any large animals—and that included humans—leave this biome.

Yoshi drew his katana. Maybe he didn't realize how small and helpless he looked compared to the giants.

The cyborgs came toward them at a jog. Armored metal feet slammed against the granite blocks of the beach and kicked aside boulders. The waves roared in from the sea.

Anna, Javi, and Crash ran toward the water, dragging their boats behind them. Molly yelled like a soccer coach, "Go go go go go!"

Akiko and Kimberly shrilly piped out the song. The difference tones fluttered in Akiko's ears. One of the cyborgs was slowing, stopping. It was confused by the music. Perhaps it heard an ancient message hidden in the hymn.

Akiko and Kimberly repeated the song, their eyes blinking in the hot wind from the sea. They hoped it was working.

The others were dragging their boats down to the water.

The nearest cyborg stopped. It put its arms down.

In a weird voice, synthesizing sounds no human had ever made, it sang back to them.

Then it froze and did not move again.

There were cheers. The others had gotten to the water. They were throwing themselves and their gear into their catamarans. They were pushing off from the shore.

Kimberly stopped playing and said something to Akiko.

Akiko looked and saw that another cyborg was still coming.

She played the ghost song again.

The cyborg did not stop thudding toward them. It blared notes back at her. They sounded angry and violent. It raised its arms and aimed its weapons at the tiny, bobbing boats. It was larger than the one that had paused near the flutes. It looked newer, taller.

Kimberly screamed and clutched at Akiko's arm. She ran for the boats.

Akiko looked after Kimberly, confused. Why wasn't it working?

Then, looking at the gleaming armor on the torso of the cyborg who stood before her, she realized: It had been more than a hundred years since Muller had first played his ghost song. Who knew what had changed in that time? Who knew what new orders this cyborg had received? Who knew what it was demanding from them, in its musical language?

Akiko moved to attract its attention. The only thing she could do was to play the song she knew and hope it would work.

She began Muller's ghost song again. But now there was no drone note to go with it.

The cyborg turned toward her.

The boats were pulling out far into the waves.

Akiko played the ancient song of farewell, hoping it would still be the key.

Her sister was screaming her name. "No! Akiko! No! Come on!"

Kira was the only other one left standing in the waves. She wouldn't push off with her boat until Akiko was safely on board.

So Akiko ran down toward her. The larger cyborg released a complicated blast of notes: a demand, perhaps—an order.

"Get on! Get on the boat!" Kira called. She was standing with one leg in the water, one leg bent in the central seed pod, holding the boat in place.

The cyborg started firing at the fleet of kids in their seed-pod catamarans. Huge plumes of water rose and fell.

Akiko hurled herself into her sister's boat and they pushed off.

Kira hectically rowed with her seed-pod paddle. Akiko struggled with hers. It bent in the water. It wasn't strong enough. It tore. They were starting to go in a circle.

"Kira!" Akiko shouted. "Row on the other side of the boat!"

Kira switched sides and they straightened out. They were headed toward the rest of the gang.

Another volley of shots hit the water and exploded around them.

And water filled Akiko's nostrils.

The boat had been hit and she was under water.

She couldn't see Kira. Couldn't see anything.

Confused green.

Couldn't breathe.

Couldn't tell which way was up. Where the air was.

Blood—her own—swirling in the sea.

Brilliant lights above—explosions heard through water.

Akiko breathed water. It sluiced into her lungs.

Nothing left. Nothing left to breathe.

She fought, punched, but there was no one there to fight.

Just death itself.

She hoped Kira made it.

By the time the cyborg got to her, she no longer saw or thought anything.

The others screamed in horror. Kira swam toward them, gasping for breath. The cyborg plowed through the water.

Hank and Crash pulled Kira up into their boat, dripping. She lay athwart them while they paddled desperately. Kira was yelling Akiko's name, wailing it almost. She wouldn't let up. "*AKIKO! AKIKO!*"

"She's gone," said Hank. "She's gone. I'm sorry, Kira. She's gone."

The cyborg lifted Akiko's body from the water and began to examine it. A new animal. An intruder to the biome. But what kind of animal?

The others were shaking. They didn't look back to see the small, broken human body.

Desperate, choking on snot, tears, and salt water, the group of survivors headed across rocking waves toward the unknown horizon.

PART 2

23

Molly

Tiny boats rocked on the huge, empty sea.

She had lost another one.

That was Molly's thought. *She* was in charge. Back after the crash, she'd been the one to suggest to Caleb he could use the device to jump above the clouds and see the stars. He was old enough to make his own decisions, but she'd encouraged him, and he'd run into tech they hadn't expected—the extra-grav setting of the alien devices. He'd been thrown down to earth and crushed.

The case of Oliver still disturbed her sleep. She'd been the one to convince his mom he should come along on the trip in the first place. After the crash, the kid had been strong, acting like it was just an adventure, but she had still been desperate to keep him safe, in particular. And instead, he'd been sucked down by the blood sand, and his body had been used as a puppet by whatever awful overlords were tracking their progress. Whatever sick game this was.

And now Akiko. Quiet, kind Akiko.

The ones who least deserved violence. They were the ones who got killed.

Molly worried that there was truth in Yoshi's bragging about the law of the jungle, the laws of strength and survival.

She and Javi rowed together, the flagship of their tiny fleet. She could feel Javi's eyes on her back, offering her support, wondering how she was doing.

How were any of them doing? Lost in a tear in the Earth, pursued by technologies that shouldn't exist for hundreds of years, fighting with monsters that should never exist at all—they were alone and stuck with one another, both attacked and abandoned.

What she would give to hear her mom say her name . . . to eat her mom's terrible mac and cheese.

Molly didn't want to be the authority anymore. She didn't want to be an adult. She wanted someone older to tell her things were okay, that the adults would take care of everything.

But she had to be the adult. She was in charge.

"We've got to eat," she said to the others. "Let's stop and eat grenade mash."

They had made a kind of paste out of the exploded flesh of the grenade fruit. It tasted zippy, but Molly could tell it had real nutrients in it—protein, in particular. She suspected it was technically a legume, like beans or peas.

Dolefully, they formed a circle with their catamarans and passed around a little pod full of red mash. Everybody got a couple of handfuls.

They ate without looking at one another and without talking.

Kira didn't eat at all. She didn't cry, either. She had fallen silent, and just sat in Yoshi's boat. She didn't row, and he didn't ask her to.

Molly ate a few bites of her grenade mash and felt sick. The anxiety was too much for her. She began to vomit into the sea.

Hank gave her a look of disgust for barfing near their meal. She wanted to say, *What? Where do you want me to go? I'm sorry, okay?*

But it was Kimberly who spoke instead. "Are you all right, Moll?" She passed her a fresh water blob. Molly took a swallow and spat to clean her mouth. She took another deep swig.

"We saw islands," she said. "We've got to reach one before tonight."

No one agreed or disagreed. When they were done eating their mash, they all kept rowing toward the far horizon.

The land where Caleb, Oliver, and Akiko had all died disappeared completely behind them.

Darkness fell and they still had not found an island.

Kira had started to row. She had noticed that Kimberly, who was alone in a boat and whose hand was still injured, was falling behind without a partner, so she'd suggested that she join her. Delicately, she picked her way across the pontoons and settled herself in front of Kimberly. Kimberly put her good hand on Kira's arm, not just to steady her while she sat, but to express her sorrow.

Cal, who was in no state to row, was squeezed into Hal and Crash's boat, muttering to himself.

Molly was worried. Hal's boat, now loaded with three boys, was riding low in the water.

Yoshi rowed alone.

The sea was a dull gray. All they had heard for hours was the crashing of the waves. In the far distance, off to their left, they could see the white line of the Arctic cliffs that marked the edge of the rift.

The fake sun dimmed and the fake moons rose. Their light glimmered across the uneasy sea, casting trails over the water, creating strange shadows.

Finally, Hank said, "Let's lash our boats together for the night."

They bound them with bungee cords and settled back to get a few hours of sleep. The moons rocked over their heads, swinging back and forth like pendulums. Molly crossed her arms and brought her knees up as far as she could. They were all scrunched up like peas in their pods. Two weeks earlier, it would have felt weird to have Javi sleeping so close to her. Now they'd all been through so much together, they were too tired to worry if it felt weird.

Molly was mainly just anxious that Javi would notice the crust and bristles growing on her skin.

"Javi?" she whispered.

He whispered back, "Yeah?"

She asked, "Can you tell me something normal?"

He thought for a second. "What do you mean?"

"Just something normal. Something you remember."

Javi considered. The boat bobbed up and down, waves lapping at its sides.

"My mom makes arepas, covered with cinnamon and way too much sugar," Javi finally said. "When we were little, every time your dad turned on a light, he'd say, 'This'll shed some light on the situation.'" Javi waited. "Is that what you're talking about?"

It was enough. Molly said, "Thanks, Javi."

"Sure, Molly. Sleep good."

She held on to those memories. Though she was cold, she didn't turn on the "battery" for warmth, because she wanted her memories to be her own. She didn't want any messages from the distant white citadel to be broadcast into her dreams. She thought about her dad, long gone, and her mom, now alone.

The swells lifted them up and dropped them down. The water rocked them all to sleep.

The moons silently swam above them.

They awoke when the roaring got loud.

Out of their separate dreams, they fumbled upright and looked out over the waves.

The red moon, the *aka* moon, was bright, and bloodied the sea.

A constant roar filled the night air. The terrifying rumble of water.

"What is it?" Javi yelled. It sounded like they were about to go over a waterfall. A little too close to home, given what Javi had told them about how the crew of the *LaRue* had gotten shipwrecked in the valley: The huge, thundering cataract, the broken whaling ship hurled into the morning air with its screaming first mate still tied to it with rope.

The sea was choppy, heaving them up and down. Molly caught spray in her eyes and mouth. She couldn't see in the ruby darkness.

"It sure sounds like a waterfall!" Kimberly shouted. "Where is it?"

Molly couldn't tell, but she thought they were being pulled forward at great speed.

Toward. Something.

She couldn't see what. There was nothing visible on the horizon. But of course it wouldn't be visible.

"We're headed right toward it!" Molly yelled. "Paddle away! Back-paddle!"

They slapped their pod paddles into the water desperately, but Molly could tell it was useless. They just spun and hurtled ever forward.

"Grab the bungee cords! Pull us in as tight as possible!" Molly ordered. She didn't want to lose anyone else.

Have to think have to think have to think . . .

Her boat swooped down a swell.

And in that moment, she saw the maelstrom. A whirlpool. They were headed right into it.

The water was white with fury.

They all were screaming alerts to one another: "In front there!" "A whirlpool!" "Back-paddle!"

The whirlpool was surrounded by a ring of roiling water, a raised wall or lip, and they were crawling up its side, fumbling toward the pit . . . about to get sucked down.

Then it hit Molly. *"Gravity sink!"* she screamed.

They were headed into one of the high gravity zones created by the little donut devices—just like, in the jungle, the circle of squat trees and unbearable weight that had killed Caleb.

Instantly, her engineer's mind drew a sketch for her: The water was flowing into a circular zone of thirty feet where it weighed double. It was plunging downward, compressed.

And then it reached the level of the device sitting on the sea floor and squirted out to the sides, flying up to create that ring of roiling water.

But that wasn't exactly how it would work for them. They'd go down into the maelstrom, weighing double, gagging on water, crushed. Trapped. The life squeezed out of them.

And by the time they shot up into the night air again, their boats would be broken, and they'd be dead.

Yoshi

Yoshi stared over the prow of his little pod boat and looked down into the eye of the whirlpool, deep and dark as a cave.

He paddled like a madman, but it made no difference. They were headed down into the gravity sink.

And this, thought Yoshi, was exactly what was always wrong. He was always tied to this group of kids, and they were always dragging him down.

This time, to his death.

Unless . . .

Over the crashing of the water, he yelled out, "WHO HAS THE ANTIGRAVITY RING? TURN IT ON!"

He saw Molly fumble in her bag. Pull out the device.

They were spinning around the edge of the maelstrom now. Picking up speed.

At any second, the extra weight would hit them.

Everyone was screaming. The boats were skidding on their sides. Yoshi gripped his boat and hoped Molly would—

Whoomf. The weight of the gravity sink hit. They all were flattened, and the water roared toward the dark center of its eye.

Yoshi caught a quick glimpse of Kira slumped in Kimberly's boat, staring into the pit as if wishing to be drowned.

Then Molly touched the symbols on the device—and everything went haywire.

Fields of gravity slammed into each other. Water jetted up around them. They went hurtling sideways.

Huge arcs of salt water flew through the red-lit air. The whirlpool vomited and gagged.

"Now row!" Molly screamed, and they all slapped their paddles into the water.

Molly still had the antigravity device on, and it was playing havoc with the waves, which sprayed into the air, almost weightless, sending the catamarans briefly aloft. They would shoot across the surface for one moment, and then would stick in the water like it was concrete.

"What's going on?" Kimberly complained.

Javi yelled back, "The friction of the water is hitting us when we have no mass! Until the gravity field—"

The water blasted ahead of them in a huge sphere, and for a sickening second, they were airborne.

"Hold on to your boats!" Molly ordered.

They slapped down.

"Going heavy!" Molly said.

With a hideous lurch, gravity hit. Yoshi reeled, close to fainting, and his stomach turned. But the sea was calmer. The roaring of the gravity sink was a long way behind them.

They didn't talk, but just kept paddling. They could feel themselves being slowly drawn backward. They had to work steadily to act against the current.

It took twenty minutes to get out of the range of the gravity sink. By that time, they were exhausted and soaked.

The clouds were growing light with artificial dawn.

Stunned by everything they'd just been through, they looked at one another. Their clothes were plastered to them. The vines holding their pontoons onto their boats were slack. The catamarans looked like they were about to fall apart.

"Good work, gang," said Molly.

That was when Yoshi noticed the shape of her shoulders in her drenched clothes.

Her skin was lumpy, and there were ridges that no human should have growing on her shoulder blades. The outline of something that looked almost like spikes or feathers jutted along her back.

She was turning into whatever Cal was. Yoshi was sickened by the outgrowths. He hated disease, and she looked like she was riddled with it. She wasn't even human. Who knew what she was?

That was it. He had had enough of this insanity.

"Hey, Molly," he said. "Want to explain your feathers?"

She looked down in the early light of morning and gasped.

When she looked up at them all, she didn't know what to say. Her mouth was open, but she couldn't speak. Everyone was silent with horror.

Yoshi felt anger flare in him. He felt like he was the one who had inhuman spikes growing out of his body: a fury that couldn't be contained. He had risked his life again and again, and it turned out their fearless leader wasn't even human.

Akiko had just died, broken at the hands of a monster for following Molly's orders. The orders of another monster. He saw Akiko's body. He could almost hear her silence. She would never speak again. Never play her sad songs on the flute again. All because this idiot was leading them around like they were on a class trip—all the while, lying to them, hiding the fact that she was turning into a beast herself. She had betrayed them. She was as bad as Hank, if not worse. And he was sick of her and her squad of schoolkids getting into trouble and then waiting for him to save them.

He was done. Absolutely done.

"That's it," he said. "I'm leaving."

Javi laughed unpleasantly. "Oh, you're just leaving?" he said. "Just leaving? How?"

Yoshi could have punched the little jerk. "By rowing away." He pointed toward the cliffs. "I'm sick of saving you."

"Saving us?" said Javi. "*Molly* saved us!"

"Only after I told her what to do."

"You didn't tell me what to do," said Molly. "Once I figured out that we were in a gravity sink, using the antigravity was obvious."

"I'm the one who said it."

"No, you aren't."

"Are you crazy? Yes, I did!"

"Well," said Molly, "if you did, I didn't hear you! I saw what was going on and got the thing out! The device!"

"I saved you all from mantis wasps. And acid slugs. And you, Anna, from the tanglevine. And all of you, from a thousand other things!" He made a high-pitched, whiny voice: "'Oh, cooperation, cooperation, let's be friends!' You're always talking about cooperation—because you need someone to protect you! And I'm sick of being that person! And then having to live with your stupid decisions when they get others killed—just like they killed Akiko!"

He began to row away, toward the distant cliffs.

"Yoshi!" Anna called out. "Come back!"

He turned and looked at her. "You're the one who knows all about biomes. So you know this: law of the jungle. Every creature for himself."

They all were pleading with him, or at least that's what it sounded like to him, floating across the waves. He thought they sounded like babies crying his name. But he didn't care anymore. He'd been living with their stupidity for too long.

He rowed for the great white Arctic wall.

Yoshi forced himself not to look back. He knew the others would be growing smaller and smaller.

His plan was to get to the edge of the rift. At night, he could pull up on the rocks. There might even be things growing there, so he could replenish his food supplies if he needed to.

Yoshi knew it would be suicide to climb the cliffs and try to set out across the Arctic wastes. Instead, he'd follow his own route toward the city of spires. But he wouldn't be obvious, like that gaggle of idiots tromping across the tundra, waving their arms and begging for mercy.

And truly, he had all their best interests in mind. He'd be able to observe what happened when the mysterious powers in charge of this place noticed them. He might even be able to get them out of danger. He, unlike them, could move swiftly and tactically alone. He was quick, determined, smart, and lithe. He could watch and wait and figure out the situation. *First, name the problem. Second, think through all the tools at your disposal. People often forget that a knife is also a mirror . . .*

His father would be proud.

The fake sun was up behind the clouds. The ocean looked wide and green, gently rocking. Far off, a sea monster played in the waves.

Yoshi was on his own.

25

Kira

Kira watched Yoshi paddle away from her and from the rest of them, and she was filled with a dull hatred. She only had a vague idea why he was leaving—she couldn't make out the conversation in English, other than Akiko's name—but she knew he was leaving her behind. He was her only link to understanding the others, the only one who could understand what she said, and he was abandoning her because he'd had some kind of a tantrum.

She couldn't believe how alone she was.

In the day since Akiko's death, Kira's heart had been as flat, gray, and cold as the sea they floated in. And like this deadly sea, she suspected her heart contained murky depths and huge monsters plowing through the gloom. She was full of crises she could not feel, drifting along on the surface like a broken doll in a toy boat, staring at the horizon because that's which way her head happened to face.

Yoshi didn't even think of her as he paddled off in a huff. He did not say good-bye to her, though he had just mentioned her sister. She could tell the other kids were calling after him and even pointing to her, probably reminding him that he was the only translator for someone whose sister had just been killed.

She was not surprised. If the rift had taught her one thing, it was that life could always betray you more violently than you had imagined. But it made a slow, quiet fire of hatred grow inside her.

For a while, she and Akiko had finally forgotten how alone they were. Sitting with Akiko and Anna on the seashore the other day, sketching, talking about teachers back at school while they watched the cyborgs guard the beach, Kira had felt hope again. It had felt almost like a fun adventure, rather than something where they risked their lives.

And she and Akiko had found new ways to be useful— coming up with the plan to make the seed pods into catamarans. Playing the flute to summon birds and stop the *kaiju* cyborgs in their tracks.

Akiko had been so proud of her role in controlling the cyborgs. She and Kira sometimes felt cut off from the others because of language; but with her flute, Akiko spoke a language that transcended English, French, or Japanese. It was understood even by the birds and the alien machines. She had proven that she was as important as anyone else in the group. She had let everyone escape.

And for that, she was dead.

Kira could not get the last sight of her sister out of her mind: the little body draped like a burst balloon in the hands of the cyborg. Akiko's dead eyes had still been open. Far too much water had poured out of her slack mouth.

A thousand pictures planted themselves over that one: Akiko's mouth open when she slept. Akiko's mouth, when they were just kids, all smeared with grease and soy from eating *yaki onigiri*, which she loved. Akiko's eyes all grimy with sleep when they had to wake up early at school. (*We give up because things were so much better in Switzerland during the Meiji era.*) Akiko's eyes, opened wide with surprise and pleasure when their grandparents arrived for a visit, or crying a few days later when they left. Kira would put her arm around her and comfort her, even when they were very small. Kira was always the stronger one. Kira always protected Akiko.

But she hadn't protected her the day before. She'd swum away, certain that Akiko was following her. And, worse, desperate with fear.

She should have stayed by her sister's side. She should have died there, too, as the cyborg's laser flares blasted at their boat.

A couple of hours earlier, when they had faced the hole in the sea, Kira had stared deep into it. She had wanted to just let herself tumble out of the boat, to be swallowed in the freezing depths. She gave her silent permission to the sea to take her.

Kira had started to roll, but Kimberly caught her. Kimberly had said something nice, something American, as if she'd just saved Kira rather than ruined her plan.

And then they were flying through the air, and gravity went haywire.

So now, here they were, crossing the basin for no good reason. Heading toward who knew what. Kira paddled without thinking about it. She did not want to go forward. She could not go back.

Everywhere she looked, there was nothing: Gray, flat sea. White cliffs. And the waves slapped the side of the boat, as if repeating *nani mo, nani mo*: nothing, nothing, nothing, nothing.

Nothing.

26

Molly

They reached a chain of islands around noon. The first ones were only a few tall rocks jutting out of the water, with single trees hunched on their crests. Then the islands grew larger, with small forests on their slopes.

No one seemed very eager to go any farther, so they pulled their catamarans up on the beach. The cliffs were high, topped with blue broccoli trees and white bushes. A flock of little gas-bag bubble creatures floated by.

Without talking much, the gang tied up their boats.

Molly couldn't meet their eyes. Any of them. Javi was being extra nice to her, taking the bungee cord from her and saying, "Here, I'll tie the boat up. You go sit down." But that was worse, because she could tell that he didn't know exactly how to treat her, now that he knew she'd been hiding something.

"We achieve new excellences," Cal muttered from a face that looked like a mask of coarse feathers and spikes.

"Great," said Molly. She stomped off to check out the island's bluffs.

She had started climbing up to the island's high point when she realized she should be back with the others. It wouldn't help to be distant from them and useless. They needed to keep working together. They were all still a team.

She trudged back down.

"We need to find some more tanglevine," Hank was saying, "or something else strong enough to lash the boats together again. They're all pretty damaged."

"I never thought I'd *want* to find tanglevine," Anna said.

Everyone stared awkwardly at Molly when she reappeared. No one said a word. The silence was awful. They all just stood there, holding their sacks of grenade mash and their handfuls of *omoshiroi*-berries.

"We should probably just stay here for the night," Molly announced. "We can check out the whole island to make sure it's clear of dangers. Then we can try to stock up on stuff we need. We'll leave tomorrow morning."

That's when people stopped looking at her.

Hank stepped forward. His expression was kind, patient. It made Molly break out into a cold sweat. "Um, Molly, this is a tough thing to say, but . . . There might be a danger on the island." He frowned. "You might be it. You might be the danger. We don't know when you'll turn. You could attack us suddenly. Or be sending messages of some kind."

Molly felt like he'd punched her in the chest.

"You understand what we mean," he said. "We don't know exactly what to"—Hank's eyes flicked to Cal, then back again—"expect."

"What to expect from what?" Molly narrowed her eyes.

"From you." Hank looked at his feet. "We don't know what you and Cal are."

"That's ridiculous," said Javi, moving over to Molly's side. "Hank, that's stupid. We know Molly's the same person mentally. Whatever's happening to her, she's still Molly."

Hank held up his hands apologetically. "No, Javi. We don't know that."

"We're not being mean, Molly," Crash said. "It's just what's true."

"What are you saying?" Molly said. She felt both like crying and like screaming at them. "What are you going to do?"

"We want a new vote to see who runs the group," Hank said.

"You're talking about 'we,' but who's 'we'?" Anna demanded. "I don't want a new vote. Molly's in charge of Team Killbot. Even if she's turning into some kind of new life-form."

Molly was glad that Anna stuck by her, even if she didn't need to hear the extra bit about her transformation.

"So a vote's only fair," said Hank. "If more people vote for Molly, then we'll all stick with Molly."

Angrily, Javi said, "And if more people vote for—just as an example—Hank? What happens then?"

Hank ignored the sarcasm. "Then I'll be the leader for a while."

"Forget it," said Javi, and started to stalk away into the woods.

"Don't leave," Hank warned him. "It'll just be one less vote for Molly."

Steaming, Javi returned. "How are we going to explain this to Kira?"

Kira had been lying on a rock, staring at the horizon. At the sound of her name, she turned. Her eyes were as blank as the sea, and just as uninterested in the group's fate.

Still, Kimberly said, "I can do mime to let Kira in on what's going on. And Javi, Anna, Molly, you've got to understand—we don't know you as well as you know one another. You've all been friends for years. But we only met you a few days ago. We wouldn't be able to tell if Molly's personality was changing."

"Hank had this all planned out," Anna announced. "Not about Molly turning into a cryptid—he didn't know about that—but about taking over. He was talking about it with Crash. Akiko, Kira, and I heard them."

Crash looked shocked that he'd been caught.

Everyone started yelling at one another.

"You're just trying to take control!"

"I'm just trying to protect us!"

"Molly's not some kind of monster!"

"Actually, she sort of is."

It got worse and worse until Molly yelled, over them all, "*STOP IT!*"

They fell silent.

"I'm stepping down as leader," Molly said. "We've lost two people in just one day. This isn't worth fighting over. What's important, now that Akiko and Yoshi are gone, is that we all stick together."

Everyone looked relieved, and for a brief moment Molly actually felt better. She was free of all that guilt and responsibility. She was done concealing her transformation. This was the right thing to do. She should have told them days ago.

Until she saw Hank's face. He looked too smug, as if he was trying to hide how good he'd felt that he won.

None of us has won, Molly thought. *Not until we're out of here.*

That night, they made a bonfire on the shore of the island. They heard something bellowing at them from a distant shore, but it came no closer.

Molly felt sick to her stomach. She missed home so much it hurt. It didn't matter that at home, she and her mother were all alone. She wanted to be back in the city, where there were the sounds of people playing in the park every morning, and where there were taxicab horns at night; where there were TV series to stream and movie endings to argue about, and her mother could say to her, "Molly, you're doing great. Love you."

Javi came and sat by her side.

He didn't say anything. She didn't know whether he was trying to respect her silence, or whether he, too, wondered what she really was becoming.

Their fire was a tiny spark of light in the vast ocean of night.

27

Yoshi

Yoshi paddled along the Arctic cliffs, watching strange, lumpy seabirds circle far above him.

The morning was bright—as bright as it ever got in this strange world, where daylight was always filtered through the clouds.

He was glad he had slept on the rocks at the base of the cliffs. Around midnight, the rift's night wind, the *yokaze*, had swept across the ocean, and huge waves had crashed against the shore. He found himself hoping that the others weren't floating in the middle of the sea, defenseless when the cold wind hit.

Now the morning was quiet. He rowed his catamaran past huge blocks of granite and tumbling waterfalls.

Through the skin of the pod, he could feel the water was frigid. Of course it would be. Minutes earlier, it had been meandering past glaciers, through snow fields, and under icebergs. Up there in the normal world.

He wished he could scale those cliffs. But even if he could, he'd be trapped in the Arctic.

His eye followed the top of the cliffs like a hawk's. Much farther along, he could see activity: It looked like the little robot mites were climbing up and down, working on the rock. He figured they were probably stabilizing it somehow, making sure it didn't collapse.

He watched them as he quietly paddled closer, bobbing on the waves.

He was not looking down, therefore, when eyes deep below spotted him. He didn't notice the dark, hungry mouth that rushed up toward him.

Something slammed into the bottom of Yoshi's boat, hard. For a second, the world spun in front of his eyes. He struggled to hold on to his paddle.

Nothing broke the surface. He peered down. Just waves. Then a dark shape.

The boat jolted upward again. For a hideous moment, Yoshi was almost thrown out of the seed pod—he flailed—gripping the paddle tightly with one hand while gripping the gunwales with the other. There was a crack. The sticks holding one of his pontoons on had broken. The boat was sagging into the water—and something huge was circling it.

The head rose slowly: something like a killer whale, but nothing like a beast on Earth. It was whiskered and feathered like a dragon, but had no eyes, just dim, sensing globs that waved as it surfaced. Its mouth was open, and the sunlight glinted on bristling teeth.

No time to get out the katana. Yoshi would have to find another way to fight.

The tail flipped, sending a huge wave at his boat. Panting, Yoshi scrambled to remain upright as water coursed over his pod.

With a convulsion of muscles longer than a pickup truck, the death whale lunged.

Yoshi back-paddled, yanking himself out of the creature's path.

It dove and readied itself for another pass.

Yoshi could see it turning in the crystalline green depths. He could see its globby sensors shuddering, weaving, and calculating.

It roared to the surface.

Its mouth hung over him—swooped down—

And Yoshi jammed the broken pontoon into its mouth, impaling it with the jagged sticks.

The creature tried to close its jaws, but one of the wooden spikes burst through its cheek. It let out a rasp in shock and pain, bleeding.

Now it couldn't open its mouth wider or shut it entirely. It locked and unlocked its jaws. It gagged and convulsed.

Blinking, the monster sank. Yoshi watched its shadow plow away through the waters.

He floated, panting, covered in the monster's blood. For a long time, he didn't move much, but just surveyed the waves.

When he was convinced the thing was gone, he started to relax.

Sure, Dad, try to ground me. Try to punish me for stealing that blade. Do you understand that I'm a warrior now? I've fought enemies more terrifying than anything seen in the age when that sword was forged.

His boat was ruined. It sagged lopsided in the water. The pod he sat in was deforming with his weight. It was torn, and frigid water was splashing over the lip. Now that the adrenaline rush was dying down, Yoshi was all too aware that his clothes were soaked and ice-cold, and he was about to get a lot wetter: His other pontoon was almost unfastened.

He didn't know what to do. He felt tired. He wondered if he should land at the foot of the cliffs for a few minutes and rest. Maybe he could repair the boat. Unfortunately, nothing was growing on the rocks.

There was no sign of life but the little robots, clustering like ants along fault lines in the stone.

Yoshi knew he was in trouble. Akiko's idea for pontoons had been an important one: Without support, these pods were too weak to hold up for long. He had a choice between stranding himself on the rocks or trying to continue onward and eventually sinking.

He might die alone in this alien sea.

There was nothing for it but to get to shore. Maybe, just maybe, there would be some way to climb along the rocks sideways across the base of the cliffs until he reached the next biome. It could only be three miles or so—less than an hour's walk, if he could walk on water.

Walking on water. There were some skills his dojo hadn't taught. He smiled to himself.

And he started to row toward the nearest cliff.

The boat felt tired and broken. It dragged with every sweep of his paddle. Every few strokes, a wave would burst over the top. He had to stop to bail himself out with the scoops of his paddle. He was shivering.

Doggedly, he kept rowing for shore.

A buzz drew his attention.

Not another monster . . .

No—he saw now, it was a boat. A motorized boat. White, with curved fins and spikes like no boat he had ever seen.

It was leaving from a rocky inlet right below the column of climbing mites. It was headed in his direction.

Yoshi took a deep breath.

Here was his chance to find out who was in charge of this place.

All he had to do was get run over.

The boat zipped along the water, maybe twenty feet long, but hardly touching the waves. He realized that it must have some antigravity element in its drive. Certainly, the water under it was acting weird. The craft must be pushing itself up and forward somehow with a gravity field.

That was good. It made it more likely he'd survive.

He rowed furiously in an arc to intercept it—or, more exactly, so that *it* would intercept *him*.

It zipped along, puffs of water breaking under its hull.

There was a chance the captain, whoever and whatever it was, would see him and stop. That could be good, could be bad.

Yoshi wasn't counting on it, however. He suspected that from a distance, he and his pontoon boat looked like vegetable trash.

The prow of the strange boat was getting closer. Yoshi slapped his paddle into the waves, trying to drag himself into the craft's path.

He couldn't see any windows or an obvious bridge. Now he suspected no living creature was aboard. *Robots*, he thought exasperatedly. Yoshi was getting nearly as tired of robots as he was of monsters. Mites, cyborgs, claw robots . . . And Team Killbot itself. *I never want to see another robot. People should just do their own work. And their own killing, too.*

The boat slid toward him. With the craft flying along at that speed, he'd only have one chance. It was not going to be easy . . . And the motorboat better be using antigravity technology, because otherwise Yoshi's arms would be torn from their sockets.

The boat was almost right next to him.

He steeled himself.

Not yet . . . Not yet . . . NOW!

He leaped out of his catamaran, sending it warping backward—but hurling himself into the motorboat's antigravity field.

For a second, he felt almost weightless. Accelerating quickly in the same direction as the boat. His stomach fizzed with sudden lightness. He swam through the air.

He grabbed on to a strut.

Weight hit. Tore at his clamped fingers. Punched at his stomach. His heart reeled. He gritted his teeth.

Pulled himself up. Water slapped at him from below.

He was hanging on to the side of the boat.

Trembling with the effort, Yoshi pulled himself up. He threw a leg over the side and scissored himself onto the top of the craft.

No obvious way in. He crouched among strange fins that looked as if they were made to negotiate different liquids than water.

He was soaked and freezing.

He looked back in the motorboat's wake and saw the shell of his catamaran swirling and sinking, torn apart.

He braced himself against the hull. He watched the waves shooting past beneath him.

It was not a bad place to be, with the sea wind blowing in his hair. His shirt was drying, stiff with salt.

Five minutes later, the boat was zipping toward an island, a huge rocky outcropping in the middle of the sea. Vehicles crawled across the granite, and in the air above it, small egg-shaped craft rose and fell. And on the highest peak, a slender, white tower rose, glistening in the daylight.

Yoshi felt a thrill go through him. In a few seconds, they'd be docking on that island.

He had a feeling he was about to get some answers.

28

Javi

"Give me the device, Molly," said Hank. He held out his hand to take it. His tone reminded Javi of a mom demanding a toy from a naughty kid.

Javi hated it.

"Stop it, Hank," said Javi. "Molly can keep it."

"I think it's only fair that the leader of the group controls the device," Hank insisted.

They were gathered on the beach under the dawn skies, just about to set out from their island in their repaired boats. But first, they had to agree about who carried what.

Molly looked shocked that Hank was demanding the device, perhaps even frightened. Javi couldn't stand to see her like this. She had been so sure of herself as a leader. Javi had loved her confidence. He'd admired her more every day. And now it seemed like she had crumpled. She held her pack protectively, with the device shoved away deep in its pocket.

"Come on, Moll," said Crash. "Give him the thingy so we can get going."

Javi stepped forward and said to Anna and Molly, "We can leave this island without giving Hank anything. We just need to get in our boats."

"That's not fair," Hank said.

"It's totally fair," said Javi.

"It's nothing personal," Hank explained to Molly. "It's just, we don't know if we can trust whatever you're turning into."

"Really?" Javi protested. "Well, Hank, we know for a *fact* we can't trust *you* with the device, right? You've already proved that, remember?" He grabbed Molly's arm in one hand and the rope for their boat with the other and marched them toward the water. He shot back to Hank, "Or are you too old to remember? Maybe your memory is going, gramps?"

Hank rushed him, his face full of rage.

Javi hadn't been in a fight for years. But now everything hit him at once—all the danger, all the pain, all the unfair torture that never let up for one minute in the rift: the slashes from shredder birds; Oliver's innocent, undead eyes when he was resurrected as a puppet; Caleb's broken body; the stings of exploding fruit; the terror of hungry sand; and the challenges now to Molly as a leader—especially that—because that was the most unfair thing of all. Molly's transformation.

And suddenly, Javi's veins were as full of red anger as Molly's were of alien infection, and he punched Hank in the face.

Hank was a better fighter. He grabbed Javi's fist and twisted his arm. The two lurched sideways, struggling. Javi's anger was so huge he felt like he should be able to obliterate Hank. He struggled in Hank's hold.

"Hey! Stop it, you guys!" Kimberly ordered. "Stop it!"

With his free hand, Hank jabbed Javi in the gut and ribs, blow after blow. Javi couldn't breathe. He felt like he was going to throw up.

But he was too mad to give up. He slackened for a second, and then lunged. He and Hank toppled onto the beach. Hank rolled them over and forced Javi's skull sideways, burying half his mouth in sand. Javi kicked upward with his knee. It wasn't a classy move, but it was effective. Hank bellowed in pain and doubled up. He dropped to the side.

"Stop it!" Kimberly yelled again. "You two are acting like ten-year-olds!"

Javi was out of breath. He'd forgotten fighting took up so much energy. Slowly, he crawled to his knees, then to his feet. Everyone stood around, looking guiltily at the two of them. Hank was just starting to uncurl.

"That was low," Hank groaned.

Javi didn't say anything. He went over and grabbed Molly's wrist and led them to the water. The two of them got in their boat.

"Anyone else coming?" said Javi.

"Me," said Anna.

Molly wasn't looking at anyone. She was clearly ashamed.

She dug in her backpack and pulled out the device. "Here," she said, and handed it to Anna.

"You don't need to give it to me," Anna protested. "Honest. I trust you."

"Thanks, Anna," said Molly.

"Don't trust her," Hank warned Anna. "She's not herself anymore."

Cal turned to Hank, his strange eyes wide. "We're your friends . . ." he mumbled. "Molly and me. We're your friends."

He shook his distorted head in disgust. "Jacks on the sidewalk."

"Come on, Cal," said Anna. "No one understands what you're saying, unfortunately. No one knows who Jack is. Get in. We're going. Maybe you could try to row today. Kimberly, Crash, Kira, are you coming or staying?"

"Jacks on the sidewalk," Cal repeated to Hank, like an accusation. "We played jacks on the sidewalk. As little kids. You know me. Hank knows Cal. Birthdays. Best friends. Halloween. *Creature from the Black Lagoon*. A monster. Behind the mask: me. Looking for candy. That's all. Two friends: Hank and Cal. Two best friends."

"Sit down and take the oar," Anna told him.

"Paddle, actually," said Cal. He still stared right at Hank. "Summers at Lake Hotchkiss. Canoes. The raft. Diving. Two friends: Hank and Cal."

Hank was standing motionless on the shore. Kimberly and Kira readied their boat for launch. "We're all coming with you," said Kimberly. "We're going to stick together."

"Come on, buddy," said Crash, tugging Hank's elbow. "Let's go."

Hank was staring at the mutated Cal sadly. Thinking, maybe, about two best friends who had lived in Oregon fifty years before.

Hank looked like he felt like garbage, and Javi was glad. He and Molly rowed away from the island.

Hunched in Anna's boat, Cal still didn't row. Anna grunted with effort as she pushed off from shore and rushed to get in behind him. Cal just kept talking. "Hank and Cal. Always over at Cal's house. Listening to records. Hank wants to be a great composer. Playing records and talking about music.

Hank writes a song for Lake Hotchkiss. He writes it on the piano. We sing it in the canoe."

Anna was having trouble keeping up. Javi slowed his paddling so that she and Cal wouldn't fall behind. Kimberly and Kira pushed off just behind them.

But then Cal stuck his paddle in the water and started to heave away, singing in a weird, warbling voice: "The water is blue, the skies are, too. And red is the meat on the barbecue . . ."

"Now, that is an amazing song," Javi muttered to Molly. "Hank really is going to be a great composer. Just like Beethoven or Mozart. The barbecue song will live forever."

Hank just stood on the bank, listening to the song he'd written a half century before at Lake Hotchkiss. Crash didn't say anything, but kept on readying the last boat for the two of them.

"Then," said Cal, "we flew through the sky across the lake to meet Carol Lombardi. She thought you were cute. We joked." He started singing again, crooning in his weird, alien voice: "The water is blue, and Carol is cool, where she sits on her seat by the side of the pool . . ."

"This is just getting better," said Javi bitterly. "I wish my phone still had some juice. I'd love to record this for YouTube and future generations."

Molly didn't answer him. She was sitting in front of him, just rowing. He couldn't see her face.

He could see her back, though, and it was shaggy with spines.

Javi tried not to think about it. He just rowed.

For most of the morning, Javi and Molly had stayed close to Anna and Cal, but about twenty feet away from the others. Javi was trying to pretend Hank wasn't there.

Once, Javi called back to Kira and Kimberly, "Come on up here with us!"

But Kimberly was too loyal—or too much of a peace-maker—to break away from Hank completely. Kira just stared into the distance, either not hearing him or pretending not to.

In truth, Hank and Crash were the best at rowing. They easily could have lapped everyone else. But they hung back, trailing slowly behind. Javi hoped it wasn't some annoying watchful-leader garbage.

"I wonder what's happening to the Yosh-bag," Javi said conversationally. "Do you think he made it to land last night?"

Molly said, "Don't call him 'Yosh-bag.'"

"Yosh-bag isn't here to hear me call him Yosh-bag." Javi kept on rowing.

"Javi . . ."

A few minutes later, Hank and Crash were cruising up beside Anna and Cal. Hank asked them, "How are you doing? Everyone okay?" as if it were just a routine check-in by the boss.

Then Hank pulled up to Javi and Molly and kept even with them. Javi just stared straight ahead at the horizon. He kept rowing.

"I'm sorry, Molly," said Hank. "You understand, though."

"She understands you're being a jerk," said Javi.

Kira pointed and called out, in English, "Look! Look!"

They all looked where she was pointing.

There, on a distant island, a column of black smoke had started to crawl into the sky. It was thick and industrial. There was nothing natural about it.

"Okay, everyone," Hank ordered. "We're going to head for that island. We want to see what this is."

"Of *course* we are," said Javi.

"I'm just saying, that's what we should do," said Hank.

"We know that's what we should do," said Javi. "Because it's obvious. You don't need to tell us."

"I'm not 'telling' anybody. I'm just suggesting that—"

He didn't get any further than that. Because all around them, huge globes burst from the water, screaming with a terrifying, high-battle squeal.

Javi could barely understand what he was looking at. They were creatures like none on Earth—a little similar to the flocks of floating gas-bags on shore. They had blunt tentacles or pseudopods, and they thrashed and bumbled toward the kids' flotilla.

Javi yelped with surprise but moved quickly, smacking one of the green beasts away with his paddle. Another bobbed up in its place, also squealing out of an ugly little hole.

As Javi battled it with his oar, several more creatures leaped from behind. They were clustered on him, their wet, mossy fingers fumbling across his face.

Then the stinging started. Pain jolted through Javi's skull, down his neck, and into his arms. Their clammy, greenish flesh was shoved against his nose and mouth. He could barely breathe.

Wham! Molly hit a couple of them away with her paddle. She raised it up to confront the next attackers.

Javi couldn't believe her strength. Several bubble creatures went flying. One popped with a hideous, wet smack; it deflated in midair and dropped dead into the sea.

Javi gasped for breath. "Thanks, Molly!"

She stood in their pod boat, wielding her paddle like a sword, a fierce look on her face.

And then more orbs overwhelmed them, leaping from the water onto the boat.

It tipped, and Javi found himself under the water.

The spheres moved in for the kill, their tentacles squirming.

29

Yoshi

The low-gravity motorboat skipped across the waves and docked itself at the mysterious isle. Yoshi had trouble holding on: Clearly, the antigravity field wasn't made for the benefit of stowaways. Even slight shifts in his weight almost threw him into the water.

He held on for a moment after the boat came to rest on a platform. He wanted to see what happened before he revealed himself.

Yoshi had still been half expecting the top of the boat to open like a lid, revealing some kind of pilot. Instead, a panel must have slid aside on the belly of the boat, because it began dropping ranks of the brick-size mites onto the landing platform. There were twenty or thirty of the little robots, all carrying long, tubular instruments with their wiry whiskers.

Without any hesitation, they marched off uphill.

Yoshi let out his breath. He slid to the side of the boat. It was about ten feet to the ground. He gripped one of the fins, or wings, or whatever—and lowered himself down until he was dangling by his arms, then dropped the final few feet.

No one was around.

Identical boats were spaced along the platform, ready to fly off across the sea.

Farther up the hill, gangs of mites marched on unknown errands.

Yoshi flipped from the side of the boat and started to climb toward the white tower. He saw strange craft hovering beside it, moving up and down. One darted off toward the horizon— in the direction of the distant city of spires.

None of the armies of mites paid any attention to Yoshi as he pulled himself up the rocks. They clearly had been programmed to ignore local animals—and that's all Yoshi was to them.

He was very aware, however, that the mites could change their attitudes fast. He'd seen it happen. At the border to the desert of blood sand, they'd turned on Javi like an angry mob. They'd sicced a pincer bot on Yoshi himself, and he'd barely escaped with all his limbs intact.

Yoshi crouched low as he climbed the rocks. He tried to shield himself from the thin tower. He didn't know whether he wanted to attract attention or not. First, he wanted to figure out what was going on.

Up the slope, a larger, six-legged machine—either a vehicle or a robot—grappled with cubes of rock, carrying them along a ridge. Yoshi couldn't see a cockpit or a driver.

What if this whole facility was simply overseen by robots?

There was a huge roar from the other side of the island. Yoshi fell flat against the boulders and looked around.

The roar continued. It sounded industrial.

Seconds later, a plume of thick black smoke rose up into the sky.

Yoshi picked his way up to the crest of the island. He saw other six-legged contraptions, looking as much like insects as machines, clambering around the rocks. They didn't pay him any attention. He made his way with as much stealth as possible. Somehow, he didn't think anyone would care that he was there.

He reached the crest of the island, and looked down on the other side.

He saw now that the stone was being mined or quarried. A huge chunk of the island was missing from the other side. There was a gargantuan pit with straight, sheer walls.

The tower was slender and white, knobbed with weird black bulbs, like cankers or pustules on a tree. At its base was some kind of a facility, built in a strange domed style of architecture Yoshi had never seen before. It had no windows. The smoke was pouring out of the domes on the far side of the building.

Mites were swarming all around the mining pit. Hovering vehicles dropped down, clearly using low-gravity tech to lift chunks of rock that must have weighed twenty or thirty tons. They deposited them into a hopper in the domed building, where the hunks of rock were pulverized with flashes of light.

Time to find out what was happening inside that building.

Yoshi shimmied down a cliff and made his way toward the complex.

There were no doors on the set of buildings—at least, not doors made for humans. There were clearly hatches that would slide open for vehicles. There was no sign of life, except a quiet flock of the balloon creatures, which floated by on the wind, blown across the sea from another island.

As he lowered himself down and crept closer, Yoshi found himself wishing that Anna was there. Somehow, he thought she'd have something useful to say about the behavior of the robots. They made a good team.

Just a couple of nights before, they'd been sitting there by the fire, talking about swordsmanship and the art of breathing. He really could use her now, standing by his side, whispering stuff she knew so they could plan.

An egg-shaped thing was drifting down toward him from the slender tower. Something like a drone, he suspected. It picked up speed. Yoshi figured it had spotted his movement.

It was now or never.

Setting his face firmly, Yoshi raised a hand in greeting.

The sphere approached, hung in the air thirty feet away, and inspected him.

He waved.

At that, there was a grinding noise, and a pincer bot appeared over a nearby rise, guided by the drone. Its claws were open. It crawled toward him.

"That's how you want to play?" Yoshi said, and he drew his katana.

He stood at the ready. He'd let the robot come to him.

As it approached, he gave a few practice swings. But that was stupid, of course. He stopped himself and adopted a neutral posture, *chudan no kamae*, that could be used for attack or defense. Mentally, he prepared himself to strike the robot's head, an ancient move that would—

A brilliant light shot down from the drone and blasted him sideways.

By the time he hit the stony ground, Yoshi was paralyzed and defenseless.

As the pincer bot approached, Yoshi's numb hand relaxed, and the katana slid from his grip. When the fatal machine reached him, he was unconscious.

30

Anna

With horror, Anna watched the pack of water spheres tip over Javi and Molly's boat. Dozens of the spheres bobbed to the surface, crawling all over each other blindly, fumbling for human prey. Kira and Kimberly were ferociously fighting them off with paddles. Hank was shouting orders that no one could hear or follow. "Someone get over to Molly and Javi! Pronto! Someone get over and pull them out of the water!"

Anna watched him row toward the swamped boat—but he was blocked by the roiling water spheres. The second they felt the tap of his boat's prow, they started to squirm and flail up toward him.

"Cal!" Anna yelled. "Could you please help me row toward Javi?"

But even as she drove her oar deep into the water, paddling with all her might, the analytical part of her brain—that part that never stopped working and often got her in trouble—was digesting what she saw.

The bubble blobs crawled up the pontoons of Hank's boat, slapping with their short tentacles.

"They're blind!" she shouted. "These creatures are working by feel!"

So how did they know we were here in the first place? she wondered.

She dug in her paddle and rowed. "Javi!" she shouted, watching him desperately try to tread water. "Javi!"

He grabbed one of the pods from his boat, but it had turned over and filled with water, so it just sank. Orbs rose around it, screaming. The sound was hideous.

Javi began jolting, shocked electrically, or poisoned maybe, by the tips of the monsters' tentacles. He couldn't keep treading water.

He disappeared beneath the waves.

Desperately, Anna worked her way toward him.

Molly was doing much better than Javi. She didn't seem to be bothered by the tentacles. For some reason they weren't shocking her in the same way. (*Alien immunity? Later!*) Molly's teeth were gritted in anger. She knocked spheres away with her fists, bashing them with surprising strength.

Anna was almost at Javi's side.

Now she was encountering something else . . . Thin little threads were spread throughout the water all around them. Her paddle picked them up and threw them aside. The threads twitched.

Suddenly, the orbs knew she was there. They began to mob her boat. Cal made a weird, moaning sound.

Anna kicked at them.

The orbs could feel things, and they worked their way toward whatever moved. But it was more than that . . . When this pack of spheres was on the ocean floor, there must be a way for them to recognize from a distance what was alive and what was just moving because of the currents. How did they recognize living things?

Javi, wide-eyed and panting, slapping desperately at the water, appeared by the side of her canoe. He winced as another sphere stung him. "*Aah!*" he cried out, and he reached a flailing hand up for help.

Anna grabbed it and began to pull him up from the water.

Spheres jumped all over her back.

She almost dropped both her paddle and Javi when the stinging started.

It spread like a spiked flower through her shoulder, down her arm, across her back. She arched and gasped, then elbowed one of the pawing spheres off her. It rolled backward and plopped into the sea—but another was already crawling over it, squealing.

Javi was gagging on water. Anna yanked on his arms as hard as she could. His face looked frightened but hopeful, as if she might save him.

"Cal? Could you give me a hand?" she asked. Cal turned and took one of Javi's arms, and started hauling him up.

Anna was shocked at Cal's strength. He was singing a phrase over and over again. It didn't have words, but just sounded like twittering. It was short. He pulled and sang.

For a wild second, Anna hoped it might be a song that would convince the sea bulbs to stop attacking them.

Javi had now grabbed on to the side of their boat. He could support himself that way, slapping at the spheres with one hand while holding on with the other.

The creatures continued the assault. Two of the spheres dived at Anna and stung her. She jumped and quivered from the shock. One of them started to paw its way toward her mouth.

Why my mouth? she wondered as she prepared to choke to death.

Suddenly, the answer came to her, and, as she spat out the monster's pseudopod, she shouted: "Heat!"

No one was listening, but now Anna knew: The spheres had some way of detecting heat. That was how they found their targets.

And so the best way to combat them would be . . .

She fumbled in her pack.

A sphere stung her face. Anna arched in pain. She was blinded.

These spheres weren't the only creatures who could work without sight, however. Eyes clenched shut in pain, Anna pulled the ring-shaped device out of her bag. Her fingers crawled along the edge, looking for symbols. She pressed two—one for less, and one she'd been hoping to try for some time now, but wasn't allowed to. She had an idea what it might do.

Suddenly, the temperature dropped.

The air got cold. The water was freezing.

Immediately, the creatures slowed their attack.

Anna shouted, "Stop moving! Everybody! Slow down!"

"*What are you doing?*" Crash yelled at her, fighting off spheres.

"They sense motion and heat!" Anna screamed at him. "Stop your stupid moving!"

Crash got it. He yelled something at Hank. Both looked wide-eyed with surprise, but they stopped moving.

Molly was still thrashing in the water, and the orbs rushed toward her in a bundle.

But for the rest of them, once they stopped moving, they were essentially invisible. The spheres could detect motion and heat. Now no one was moving much . . . and the water was rapidly cooling, no longer carrying their heat signatures.

The pack of spheres could no longer detect them.

Molly grabbed on to her overturned boat. She didn't have to tread water anymore. She just hung there, breathing heavily from the battle.

Gradually, the spheres slowed down. They stopped squealing, but rested in the nest of thin strings that trailed through the water.

What, Anna wondered, were those strings? She followed them with her eyes, careful not to move her head.

Anna could see that there was one larger sphere, more brown than green, in the center of the cluster. All of the strings led to it. They were part of it.

It was the ringleader, somehow. Some sort of queen sphere. Anna filed the fact away in case she needed it.

Everyone tried to calm themselves, though stinging death floated inches away.

What was left was a strange scene of danger: All the kids rode silently on the sea, without moving a muscle. They were surrounded by a field of spheres, all of which were waiting for a hint of heat or a quick, jostling motion so that they could attack again.

And the temperature was still dropping. With the device on, faint plates of ice were already starting to build—and this was salt water, which froze at a much lower temperature than fresh water.

Even as Anna watched, Javi started to shiver.

Oh no, thought Anna. *That's motion.* She had to stop him from shivering before he gave his position away. But also, he and Molly only had a minute or so before they froze to death.

They all drifted there together, interlocked, waiting for disaster.

Molly

Molly clung to the bottom of her boat, drifting, freezing. Her muscles were stiff. Her whole body ached with cold. She was starting to quiver.

The soup of tendrils began to drift toward her, detecting motion.

The second those tendrils touched her, all these spheres would know she was alive. And then they'd pounce.

Molly tried to stop herself from shivering. But it wasn't a choice. And she could see the little ripples circling her body, bearing news of her movement to the spheres.

Suddenly, Anna announced, "Kill the big brown sphere. We've got to kill it! It's the leader! The others can't sense anything except short-range, just what touches them. The big sphere with all the long, stringy tentacles is what's directing them!"

"Okay," said Crash. He was the closest to the big brown sphere. "Here goes . . ."

He brought his paddle down—hard.

The whole web of stringy sensors erupted, flailing out of the water. The sphere let out a deep cry of pain—and Crash and Hank were immediately swarmed by spheres.

Crash kept jabbing at the big brown one with his paddle. It was bleeding.

He punctured it.

It began to deflate.

The thin filaments in the water around them sank out of sight.

The other spheres were still able to detect whatever was right around them, however. They rolled and climbed and mobbed over the pods. Everyone punched and elbowed them away, gasping with the pain of their burning poison.

Molly was motionless. She couldn't move without sliding off into the frigid water and sinking forever.

When she saw that there was a lull in the fighting, she yelled out, "NOW FREEZE!"

Everyone knew what she meant. Once again, they held still.

Without their heat and their motion, the blind spheres couldn't find them. And their leader with its fine-tuned sensors was dead.

Everyone held their breath, doused with freezing water. Molly watched her hands grow white with crystals of frost.

The humans were drifting away from the cluster of spheres. The spheres waited blindly.

Javi said, through chattering teeth, "Maybe we could turn up the heat a little now?"

"Only a little," said Anna. She touched the symbols on the ring.

"That's nice of you," said Javi. "You're not up to your neck in freezing cold water."

"We don't want them to come back."

The spheres were starting to fumble, seeking out motion. The cluster of them moved away, fingers plucking at the waves.

"We just need to get out of their close range," said Anna. "They're a communal species, and we've killed the queen bee. No one is leading them now. Some species evolve like that, with different animals having different skills and functions. Like termites and some shrimp."

"Anna," said Javi. "I'm begging you. More heat."

"It's called eusociality," Anna offered. "When animals specialize into colonies like that."

"It's called 'You-freezing-my-butt-off,'" said Javi. "I can't hold on much longer."

Anna turned up the heat a little more.

"We have to flip our boat back over," Molly said through chattering teeth. "It's not in great shape." She looked over at Javi. "Also, I'm worried about Javi's core temperature dropping too low. We're going to have to risk warming the water."

"Really?" said Anna.

"Look at him," said Molly.

"Yeah. Look at me."

"What about you?" said Hank. "Aren't you worried about yourself?"

"I'm cold," Molly said defiantly, "but whatever I'm turning into can take cold better than humans."

Javi reminded everyone, "I'm not turning into anything except a Klondike."

"Okay," Hank ordered Anna. "Make it tropical."

Anna didn't argue. She just nodded.

Soon the water right around them was as warm as bathwater. Javi breathed a sigh of relief. They struggled with the boats for fifteen minutes, turning pods over and reattaching the pontoons with the bungee cords, vines, and rope.

By this point, they were washing toward the smoking island. They kept on paddling in that direction, but the wind was taking them along the same course anyway.

As they approached, they could see a tall, spindly tower with the egg-shaped craft moving up and down around it. In front of the island was a huge mound of discarded stone, sand, and rubble. Something was spewing rocks toward the mound. The Killbots and Cub-Tones had to be careful to avoid the path of the spray.

Once they drifted to the hill of broken rock, Molly could see a row of domes. The column of black smoke poured out of them. A chute came out of a wide entrance, and was ejecting junk gravel, sand, and boulders out over the water and into the mound.

"It's a factory of some kind," said Molly. "Maybe for making metal or something."

They rowed closer. Molly saw six-legged vehicles clambering over the rock.

Now that they were near to the shore, they could see that one of the domes had slid up, revealing its inner workings. It wasn't so much a building as a single giant machine.

"What are they making?" said Hank.

"Noise," Javi muttered.

"Might," said Kira. Confused, Molly looked over at her. Kira was pointing.

"Might what?" said Crash.

Kira turned her hand upside down and wriggled her fingers. "Might," she insisted.

Then Molly understood what she was saying. "It's a factory to make mites," she explained. "Those little robots. Look over there."

At one end of the domes, raw earth and rock was being poured into the giant machine, while the refuse was filtered out. There were giant smelting furnaces. And then parts were being assembled. Wires were spun out. Boxes were built. The mechanisms flashed in the sunlight.

"There!" said Kimberly. "They're being shipped off somewhere!" A set of mites was marching down to the docks and waiting to be picked up by a strange motorboat of some kind. They nestled into its belly like baby spiders, and it took off, bouncing across the waves.

"This is so cool," said Crash.

"We've got to keep going," said Hank. "It's too dangerous to land. And there's nothing there to help us. Just a lot of robots and rock."

"No, wait," said Javi. "We've got to land."

"Would you stop arguing with everything I say?" Hank complained.

"No," said Javi. "You don't understand. We've got to land right now." He pointed. "There's Yoshi, being dragged along by a pincer bot. And I think he may be dead."

32

Javi

Yoshi's lifeless body was slumped in the claws of the pincer bot. His limp arms dragged on the ground. The pincer bot marched along over the rocky island on its four sturdy legs. Javi tried to figure out where it might be heading.

Toward the mite factory. No . . . specifically . . .

"Come on!" Javi shouted. "It's headed for the incinerator! That smelting furnace or whatever it is! It's going to burn his body!"

They slapped their paddles into the water and headed toward the shore.

"Is he really dead?" Kimberly called.

"We won't know till we get to him!" said Javi.

"We need to make a plan," Molly insisted. "We can't just appear, or they'll kill all of us."

"Who is 'they'?" Hank said. "We don't even know who's on the island, or whose side they might be on . . ."

"Or who the 'sides' are," Kimberly pointed out. "Or what either 'side' wants."

"Stop talking!" Anna pleaded. "We've got to just go save him!"

"How are we going to stop the pincer bot?" Molly said.

"I think we should use the device," said Javi. "It can shut down tech or overload it with power."

"I thought you said that was a bad idea," said Hank skeptically. "That every time you fiddle with the power setting on one of these devices, it backfires."

"Yeah . . ." said Javi. "I almost got killed a couple days before we met you." He kept on digging his paddle into the waves. Through gritted teeth, he said, "That's why I have a plan."

They didn't wait for the prows of their pod boats to touch ground. Javi leaped out and together they dragged the boats toward the rocky shore, plowing through the water. They ran, leaving the boats grounded. Their wet shoes slapped against the rocks.

Javi sped as quickly as he could up the slope toward the factory and the pincer bot.

As they got close to the rumbling, roaring facility, sets of mites walked out to meet them, all in straight lines.

A loud fluting noise sounded through the air.

"What is that?" Hank said.

"It is a warning," Cal answered.

Javi wondered how much Cal could understand of the musical language of whatever world-builders had trapped them here. He wondered whether Molly would be able to soon. He looked over at her, running by his side, her neck scabbed with green, and worried about how long she would still be the Molly he knew.

A stream of mites poured out of the factory. They started marching toward the kids—and suddenly Javi didn't feel so good about sprinting in their direction.

The pincer bot didn't pause in its ramble toward the furnace. It carried the lifeless human animal in its claws, preparing to dispose of it. The mites would take care of the intruding figures who were scampering up the slope.

"The mites are in our way!" Anna screamed. "We won't be able to get to Yoshi in time!"

The pincer bot was only twenty feet away from the glowing furnace. Inside, flames roiled. Given the temperatures necessary for smelting, Javi figured it could easily be a couple thousand degrees Fahrenheit in there.

Yoshi, alive or dead, would be ash in seconds.

The kids came to a halt. Lines of mites blocked their way.

It was now or never.

The pincer bot stalked closer to the flames.

33

Anna

As Anna ran up the beach, she looked at Yoshi in horror. He hung slack in the robot's pincers. His eyes were closed and his mouth was open, and strings of drool dropped from his lips down onto the rocks. His head bobbed in time with the pincer bot's steps.

Now his skin reflected the red of the furnace's flames. Dark clouds of ash spread above them all. The mites stood ready to defend, their antennae twitching.

The pincer bot was almost at the furnace door.

It was time. Because there was no time left.

Anna held up the ring-shaped device. She touched the symbol to drain tech of power.

This had been a disaster the last time they tried it, when they were on the far side of the blood-sand desert: The mites were programmed to resist capture by self-destructing when they were shut down.

And that was exactly what was needed now.

Anna waited for the power drop to take effect.

For a second, the mites all went motionless.

Then they began exploding.

Rows upon rows of them burst. The pieces skittered through the air.

Anna felt nothing but joy. She usually hated the death of robots, but not in this case. She felt only the power of striking back against whatever it was that had stranded them here, whatever it was that had killed hundreds of people without reason, whatever it was that at once watched them and tormented them. The explosions felt good. The concussions rocketed through her body like music.

And even better: The kids could hear, inside the factory, the sound of mites bursting on the assembly line.

This was Javi's plan—not just to create a diversion, but to create a disaster big enough that the pincer bot dropped Yoshi and came for *them* instead.

It lay his body down and jogged toward them, its four jointed legs smacking against stone.

The kids split into two groups: Anna and the Cub-Tones stood right where they were, watching the pincer bot approach, attracting its attention—while the remains of Team Killbot ran in a long curve toward Yoshi's body.

The pincer bot halted right before it entered the sphere of Anna's device. *It must be able to detect the low-tech signal*, she realized.

Smoke was pouring out of the factory now—and not just from the smelting furnace. The rippling explosions of the mites inside must have sparked something.

The pincer bot noticed the movement to his side. It seemed about to turn back and intercept Javi, Kira, and Molly from grabbing Yoshi. In a few steps, it would slash them to pieces.

With a fierce yell—as crazed as she could make it—Anna charged the pincer bot, holding the device in front of her. Yoshi might have called her yell *kiai*—energy thrown against her opponent. She just knew she wanted to trap the bot inside the energy-sapping sphere.

For a second, its eye light wavered. Its arms dropped.

Anna wasn't taking any chances. She kept running toward it.

Then it regained its power. The robot sprang to life again. It must have some kind of safeguard against the energy suck.

It ran right toward her, clacking its pincers.

So Anna touched a different symbol, reversing the tech setting into a surge—way too much energy. When Molly had tried this before, the device had overtaxed the machinery around it, destroying what was left of the plane.

"Short circuit!" Anna screamed triumphantly, which she guessed was about as fierce as a robotics nerd could get.

But then she looked down in surprise. The device wasn't responding to her request. Instead, it was pulsing green. A set of symbols crawled along its surface, flashing. It did not look good.

She pressed other symbols. Nothing worked. The device just flashed.

There must be an override that the pincer bot tripped, she realized. *Something that stops the device from being used like a weapon.*

She was holding a useless donut of alien metal in her hand. And the robot was still rushing her.

34

Molly

When Molly, Javi, and Kira got to Yoshi's body, Molly suddenly realized that she didn't need any help to pick up the slumped corpse. Yoshi looked light to her now. Something she could carry easily. She grabbed his waist and lifted him.

Javi put his hand in front of the mouth on Yoshi's lolling head to check for breath. "He's alive!" Yoshi said.

Molly threw Yoshi over her shoulder and began jogging back down toward the boats.

She saw Anna and the Cub-Tones confronting the pincer bot.

Crash was saying to Cal, "Cal, buddy, do you know the music language for this? Can you sing to the guy? Can you get him to stop? Cal?"

But Cal was just shaking his head, eyes closed, repeating, "Maintenance is in damage mode. Maintenance is in damage mode."

Molly watched Anna try to stop the bot with their ring's low-tech setting. But the ring gave out, pulsing with a green warning light.

They had learned that in the rift, green wasn't good. It was not *Go*.

Molly knew what was going to happen: "Throw it, Anna! Throw it away! It's been locked into self-destruct mode!"

Anna's eyes widened, and she hurled the device right at the pincer bot.

Molly almost smiled to see that Anna threw it like she would throw a Frisbee. A metal Frisbee.

It slammed into the pincer bot—and the device's countdown of green flashes ran out.

It blew up.

The bot's four legs crumpled and its body collapsed, smoking and broken.

The egg-shaped craft were hovering over the scene now, spraying the factory with foam. They must be maintenance bots of some kind, Molly figured. They were trying to fight the flames.

Everyone was galloping down to the beach, and Yoshi was alive, and somehow her strong back was supporting his weight like he was nothing more than a half-full backpack. It was almost exhilarating.

They were back at the boats.

"Go go go go go!" Molly yelled, and Hank added sheepishly, "Yeah. Come on, team."

They began to paddle away from the island. Mites were pouring out of the factory now, rushing to fight the fire and repair what damage they could.

The wind was at the group's back, urging them onward. The trail of smoke led right over their heads, stretching to the far side of the basin like a line of ink being drawn across a map.

Slumped in Javi and Molly's boat, Yoshi started to wriggle and blink.

"Hey!" Javi called. "Yosh-bag! You with us?"

"What?" Yoshi said. "What's going on?"

"We just saved you," Molly explained, paddling.

"You did?" Yoshi said, shocked. "Hey, where's my katana?"

They rowed farther and farther from the fires of the factory isle.

35

Yoshi

Yoshi was furious.

His katana was back on the island. Stealing that blade had basically ruined his life, and now these idiots hadn't even bothered to save it when they saved him.

"It wasn't around anywhere," said Molly. "The pincer bot was carrying you. You must have dropped it when the bot stunned you."

"We're going back," Yoshi demanded. "Give me a boat. I'm finding that katana."

"No, Yoshi," said Molly. "We're *not* going back. We don't have any extra boats. It's too dangerous."

"The mites seem to think we're something like wild animals," Hank agreed. "If they start to think of us as actual enemies, we're screwed."

"Do you realize what that blade cost me?" Yoshi yelled.

Javi rolled his eyes. "We get the idea, Yosh-bag. Really expensive. Part of your First Class lifestyle."

"No!" Yoshi said. "Not expensive in dollars. It ruined my life."

"Well, we saved your life," said Javi, "so maybe you could stop complaining."

"I am so *sick* of you all! I'm so *sick* of going along with your stupid ideas! I'm sick of you getting in my way every time I try to do something! I don't need you!"

He looked furiously from face to face.

There was no way out. He was stranded in their sagging fleet. He couldn't head off on his own. They were all going forward.

"Maybe you better shut up now," said Hank. "We just saved you from being incinerated."

Yoshi refused to row. He was tired of playing their little-kid games, the way they turned this whole disaster into a summer camp with fun and games and activities for all. Akiko had *died* playing flute; Oliver had been taken while the Killbots played battle-bots with their stupid toy, Hercules; Caleb had died looking at the stars. All summer-camp electives that turned deadly. Stupid mistakes made by stupid kids.

Yoshi wasn't going to play along.

"There's one law of the jungle," Yoshi proclaimed, "kill or be killed. Eat or be eaten. Predator or prey." It made him feel stronger just to say it, just to tell them the truth. He wanted to hurt them, to show them how childish they were. "Every man for himself. That's the law of nature." He turned to Anna. He and Anna understood each other. "You know what I'm talking about, right, Anna?" he said. "That's the law of nature, right? Survival of the fittest."

She stared right at his eyes. He knew she agreed with him. So he was surprised when instead, she said furiously, "No, that's not right, Yoshi. That's not the law of the jungle, Yoshi!

We saved you, you jerk, because the law of the jungle is also creatures working together. Herds. Packs. Species surviving by helping each other out. Have you ever heard of mutualism? Commensalism? When species have a system where they help each other? Those are the law of the jungle, too, jerk!" Anna had stopped paddling. She seemed angry enough to throw her paddle out to sea. "We got attacked by a bunch of blind sea spheres—some kind of awful community of killers—but even they worked together! Each one had its role! That's also nature, you jerk!

"We saved your life!" she screamed. "We risked our lives for you just now! All of us! Because we want you to live!" She thrashed her paddle in the water and splashed everywhere. "SO STOP TALKING ABOUT THE LAW OF THE JUNGLE AS IF YOU KNEW ANYTHING ABOUT IT! YOU DON'T KNOW ANYTHING ABOUT SCIENCE! YOU JUST WANT AN EXCUSE TO BE A TOTAL BUTT!"

Then everyone was silent on the water. The boats bobbed up and down.

Hank cleared his throat. "Keep rowing, gang," he said. "We still have a long way to go before we reach the other shore."

Yoshi thought about what Anna had said while they rowed. He ached for his sword. He could feel the empty scabbard on his back. Being without it felt like missing a limb, or having an arm trapped in a cast.

But they really *had* saved him. Molly had quietly given him the details of the encounter at the factory as she paddled. The robots had been about to throw him into the smelting furnace. To burn his body, as if he were just an animal carcass they'd found in their mine. And the group had come just in time. They'd thrown away their tech ring to save him.

Without saying anything, he began paddling.

Throughout the long afternoon, they silently rowed away. They now could see the distant shore as a black line near the horizon.

They stopped for a dinner of grenade mash. Kira passed around the sack. They all took clumps and ate it.

Yoshi climbed into Anna's boat. He sat down. "What you said makes some sense," he told her.

"Thanks."

"Am I really a total butt?"

"Yes."

He smiled. "I guess that's better than half a butt."

Anna, chewing her mash, looked serious as she said, "I told you, Yoshi: A cluster of blind, farting spheres are better people than you are."

Yoshi couldn't help himself. He let out a spurt of laughter.

"What? It's not funny."

Javi had overheard them, and he was laughing, too.

"What are you laughing at?" Anna looked confused, but she smiled tentatively.

Yoshi liked her smile.

"From one blind, farting sphere to another," he said, and held out his hand for a high five. "Peace?"

She gave him a high five, a little too hard.

Then their fingers closed around each other. Just for a second. Yoshi wanted to keep holding her hand.

But everyone was watching. It was too embarrassing. Both of them pulled back.

He could tell, though, that Anna was blushing.

They kept rowing toward the nearest shore.

There was no choice but to go forward with them, Yoshi realized. Here was this group of science dweebs and band-camp nerds confronting an alien menace like none the Earth had ever known before. There were nine of them left. Two of them were turning into something inhuman. They couldn't agree on who was in command. Their chances for survival seemed almost zero.

And yet, they'd gotten this far by thinking hard and fighting hard. By having each other's backs.

They were going to make it. Yoshi was determined. They were all going to get out. No more dead. No more left behind.

They would stand side by side. They would stand up for each other. And they would defeat whatever unknown challenges lay ahead.

As evening fell, a mist rose from the trapped sea. Through it, they saw the red gleam of the rising moon on some massive outcropping far in front of them. They paddled toward it. Far back over a rutted, muddy plain, they could dimly see towers of metal and crystal bristling at strange angles, as if designed for a gravity that was not the Earth's. The cluster of spires projected out of the cliff face, looking as much like geology as someone's castle or citadel. There was no sound except the wash of the waves against the bleak, barren beach. There was no sign of life. And yet this was the goal they sought, and their answers would be found here.

By the time darkness fell, they had stepped out on this new continent and were embarked on another adventure.

ABOUT THE AUTHOR

M. T. Anderson is the *New York Times* bestselling author of many critically acclaimed books, including *The Game of Sunken Places*; *Feed*, which was a finalist for the National Book Award and winner of the *Los Angeles Times* Book Prize; and the two-part Octavian Nothing saga, the first volume of which won the National Book Award. Both volumes are Printz Honor Books. He lives in Cambridge, Massachusetts.

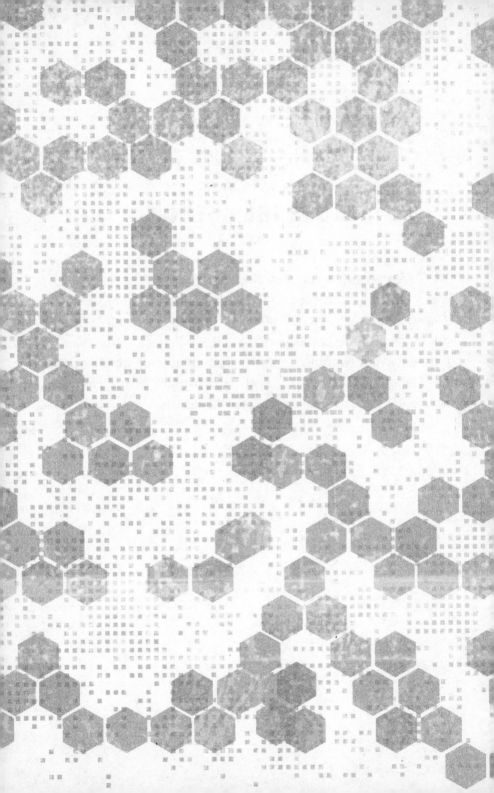

DON'T MISS

BOOK 5

HORIZON
THE GAME

A small group of survivors steps from
the wreckage of a plane . . .
And you're one of them.

JOIN THE RACE FOR SURVIVAL!

1. Download the app or go to **scholastic.com/horizon**
2. Log in to create your character.
3. Go to the Sequencer in your home camp.
4. Input the above musical sequence.
5. Claim your prize!

Available for tablet, phone, and browser.
scholastic.com/horizon

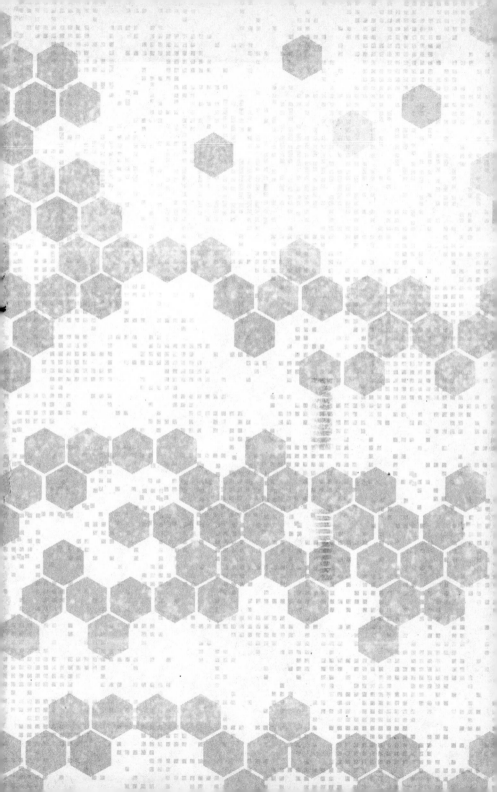